"It's starting to [...]
    Lloyd turned [...]
  fallen off her h[...]
   to touch a lock of hair that lay o[...]
      cheek. "Your hair's dry. It's curly."

She had felt so at ease with Lloyd that she had forgotten to worry about her appearance. "When my hair gets wet it always gets like this."

"It's beautiful," he said huskily, sifting his fingers through the long strands, and letting them fall onto her shoulders. "So long and silky."

"I— Thank you."

"You still have trouble accepting compliments, I see."

"I guess old habits are hard to break."

"But trying to break them can be interesting," he murmured, still running his fingers through her hair.

"I suppose," she said softly.

Taking her mug from her hand, Lloyd set it beside his and leaned toward her. Everything in the room was bathed in a soft orange glow. Behind them, the fire crackled, but Delaney saw only Lloyd as he came closer.

"Let's try," he whispered. "Then we'll know for sure . . ."

Jan Mathews

Although she grew up on a farm in a small southern Illinois town and has lived in Chicago for over twenty-five years, Jan Mathews was born in Kentucky and still calls it home. She is a wife, mother, registered nurse, and writer—sometimes in that order. With a son who has a rock band and two other children who are involved in a variety of activities, she is always busy. If she could have one wish in life it would be forty-eight-hour days. She swears that her family, as well as every volunteer organization known to man, senses that she is a soft touch. She has been active in Scouting, athletic clubs, and in the PTA.

Jan's idea of heaven would be to spend a week in the wilderness—minus poison ivy—camping and backpacking. She would love to raft the Chattooga, see the Grand Canyon on horseback, and watch Monday Night Football without being interrupted.

Dear Reader:

We're very excited to be able to offer you author Mary Modean's first book for Second Chance at Love, the deeply moving *In Name Only* (#400). Threatened with losing custody of her son Mike, Leslie Burgess flees the east coast, seeking refuge in rural Oklahoma and a marriage of convenience to rancher and veterinarian David Nichols. Sublimating past sorrows, David and Leslie work hard to pull their lives together. But he's trapped by a secret burden of pain he's afraid to share...and she's unprepared for the soul-stirring depth of desire this lean, quiet man arouses within her. Mary Modean delivers with emotionally complex characters whose compelling—and very real—love story will leave you anxious for more from this talented author.

You won't be disappointed in Liz Grady's fresh take on a "coming to terms with the past" theme in this month's *Reclaim the Dream* (#401). Washington protocol expert Laurel Forrest seems the perfect product of a classy upbringing, moving through the corridors of power with ease and sophistication...until her long-ago love, brawny maverick Sawyer Gates shows up and threatens to shatter her facade. Only Sawyer knows the lie she's built her life on, and Laurel's got to finagle her way out of being exposed. But somehow the heat of Sawyer's gaze sparks a need, and Laurel's not sure she wants to escape the danger of his strong embrace...Liz Grady leads you through a maze of love and deception to a delightfully satisfying conclusion in this, her ninth, Second Chance at Love.

Carolina Moon (#402) by Joan Darling combines exciting romance with hilarious domestic comedy for surefire entertainment. When the man of her dreams moves next door and proceeds to sweep her off her feet, Eileen "Fergie" Duffy can scarcely believe her good fortune. But her ardent neighbor, Ryan O'Donnell, has no use for children—and Fergie, a widow, happens to be the mother of three! Her kids adore Ryan, though; they unanimously decide to adopt him—and every time Ryan looks at Fergie, his resolve crumbles. The house next door starts to feel like home, and Fergie's the one woman who can make him happy...Author Joan Darling confesses she based Ryan on *Moonlighting's* Bruce Willis, and he's certainly a hunk with a sense of humor, not to mention fatal charm.

Diana Morgan exhibits more marvelous madness this month with *The Wedding Belle* (#403). Intrigued by a mysterious blonde decked out in bridal finery while she is stationed in the middle of the Chattahoochee River, patrician venture capitalist Ned Fontaine introduces himself. Soon he's introducing Jolie MacGregor to his family as *his* bride in a nonmarriage of convenience. Ned will stake Jolie as she opens a high-fashion boutique, while she'll keep unmarried Southern belles and their anxious mamas away from Ned. This perfect arrangement takes some interesting turns when Ned and Jolie fall madly in love! With the heady mist of a fine champagne, Diana Morgan presents a characteristically memorable romantic romp.

Laine Allen brings lively romance to a department store setting in *Courting Trouble* (#404), when Personnel Manager Claire Kendrick takes on an ex-convict as an employee. Mace Dawson's good looks are truly criminal—and his answers to the company questionnaire are downright impertinent. Claire's boss insists it will do this con-man good to work under her protective wing—but it's Claire's heart that needs protection when Mace starts to undo all her rules and regulations. Claire doesn't know that Mace is merely masquerading as a man in need of reform; he's actually the head of an outreach program for ex-convicts, and wants to learn how it feels to be a second-class citizen. Claire's already falling fast—and there's plenty of first-class banter as these two *try* to work together...

A widowed mother finds love again in *Everybody's Hero* (#405) by Second Chance star Jan Mathews. Delaney Anderson never wanted her seventeen-year-old son to join the Marines—and she certainly never expected to fall in love with his recruiting officer! Captain Lloyd Thomas is an officer and a gentleman, but Delaney's past with the military is a tragic one. She's afraid her years of heartbreak won't let her give in to Lloyd's sense of fun, yet he soon lures her into a schoolgirl's romance that leaves her breathless. Delaney learns to give up some of her maternal obligations, and Jan portrays her passionate rejuvenation with grace and good-natured humor. *Everybody's Hero* is another winner from an all-time Second Chance favorite, topping off a month of spring surprises.

Happy Reading!

Joan Marlow

Joan Marlow, Editor
SECOND CHANCE AT LOVE
The Berkley Publishing Group
200 Madison Avenue
New York, NY 10016

SECOND CHANCE AT LOVE™

JAN MATHEWS
EVERYBODY'S HERO

A
SECOND CHANCE AT LOVE
BOOK

Second Chance at Love books are published by
The Berkley Publishing Group
200 Madison Avenue, New York, NY 10016

A special thanks to the United States Marine Corps,
particularly Sergeant Alexander and
Staff Sergeant Frank Navratil, Jr.,
for all their help and information.

This one is for my son, Michael,
who's all grown up, too.

EVERYBODY'S HERO

Chapter 1

THE EASIEST THING about a garden would be not having one to begin with, Delaney Anderson decided as she paused to wipe the sweat from her forehead. Chicago weather was never easy to predict; even though it was only early June, the day was unseasonably hot and sticky. Delaney had been digging for several hours, trying to combat the weeds that always seemed to grow taller and faster than her vegetables.

Sighing, she pulled another prickly offender from between rows of radishes and carrots, shaking the dirt onto her bare feet. She wished Kevin were here to help her. Between his girl friend, high school athletics, and his job at the local hardware store, her seventeen-year-old son was hardly ever at home. But today Kevin *had* promised to work in the garden, and it wasn't like him not to call. Usually Kevin was so responsible, not wanting her to worry. This was the first Saturday he had taken off in months; he had left the house early this morning and hadn't come home yet.

In addition to the chores he had promised to help with, Kevin knew they were supposed to discuss which college he was going to attend in the fall. Kevin had managed to put off the decision until the very last moment, citing everything except the real reason—which was money, or rather, the lack of it. Now they had so much to do—loan papers to fill out, interviews, and if Delaney was going to double-mortgage the house, she needed to get somebody to appraise it. Maybe she ought to go to the bank herself and not wait for Kevin to come with her, she thought, yanking another weed. What could a seventeen-year-old tell a loan officer about his mother, except that she was a good credit risk even though she was a widow.

"Mom!" Kevin's sudden bellow made her start.

"Out here," Delaney answered, straightening up with a frown at the kink in her back. As long as she was taking out a loan, maybe she should borrow enough money to join the local health club. She was going to be thirty-five in a few months, and the aches in her muscles told her she was definitely out of shape.

"Mom, where are you?"

"In the garden," she called, straightening her back, "lost among the weeds."

"I told you to wait for me," Kevin answered,

rounding the corner of the shed with lanky strides. "I was going to get to it later."

"I was afraid if the dandelions got much bigger they might start to attack." Delaney smiled up at her son. Kevin was a handsome boy. Tall, blond, and blue-eyed, he looked exactly like her husband at that age. All he needed was a uniform. Delaney quickly blocked that image from her mind. Over the years she had lost so many people she loved to the service —her father, her uncle, and finally her husband had all died in the line of duty. She hated to even think about the military, for she knew that even in peacetime there was war—somewhere, for some reason, someone was always fighting.

"Speaking of attacks," Kevin muttered, and Delaney frowned as he took a deep breath and gestured toward a man who had walked up beside them. "Mom, this is Captain Lloyd Thomas. Captain Thomas, my mom."

Startled, Delaney glanced up at the dark-haired man standing beside her son. He was tall, like Kevin, but with broader shoulders and a more muscular physique, and he had the bluest eyes she had ever seen. Paul Newman eyes.

"Mrs. Anderson," he said, taking off his hat and holding out his hand. "I'm very pleased to meet you. Kevin's told me a lot about you."

His voice was naturally husky and yet honey-smooth, but as Delaney took his hand all she could think about was the formal white uniform he was wearing. It contrasted with his tanned skin and close-cropped dark hair, giving him a ruggedly masculine appearance. Yet he would have looked masculine in dress blues, too—or in just about anything, she decided. The sprinkling of gray at his temples told Delaney he was in his late thirties, but it didn't detract from the man's looks. It just gave him a rakish air, as did the elaborate gold insignia on his collar, which identified his service branch.

Delaney knew immediately that Captain Lloyd Thomas was a Marine and that he was a career officer. The military was in his stance, his talk, in the way he took off his hat and tucked it under his arm. And Delaney could also tell that he was the kind of man who volunteered for dangerous missions, a man who defied death as a matter of course, a man who was all heartache and pain. A man who had the mettle to be a Marine.

And for a moment she could only stare at him in silence, her heart pounding with dreadful foreboding. What was her son doing with him?

"Captain Thomas gave me a lift home," Kevin said, almost as though he had guessed her thoughts. "Sorry I'm late."

Why had Captain Thomas given her son a ride home? It could only mean one thing: Kevin had joined the Marines. But Delaney pushed that thought aside, along with the memories of the people she had lost. She was overreacting. Just because the man was wearing a uniform and had accompanied her son home didn't mean he had recruited Kevin. They probably knew each other in some other context.

"Where were you?" she asked Kevin, trying to smile. "I was beginning to wonder if you'd make it home for dinner."

"I was over at the shopping center."

The shopping center. The Marine recruiting station was at the shopping center.

"Actually it's my fault we're late," Captain Thomas cut in. "I had a special detail to attend and then some errands to run."

Delaney glanced back at him. She was being ridiculous. Even if the opportunity presented itself, Kevin would never join the Marines. Not when he knew how she felt about the military. The man had given her son a ride home, that was all. Besides, Kevin was going to college. "Thanks for giving Kevin a lift, Captain Thomas. I hope you didn't go out of your way."

"No problem. And please, call me Lloyd."

She smiled again. "Lloyd."

There was a brief silence while he looked at her son as though expecting him to speak. "Well," Kevin finally got out, clearing his throat, "the garden looks great, Mom."

"Thank you. I suppose I'm hired?"

But Kevin didn't laugh. Captain Thomas nodded at the hoe. "Do you need some help finishing up?"

Considering his white uniform, it was gallant of him to offer. Delaney shook her head no. "Thanks, but I think I'll quit for today. I'm tired and—" She glanced down at herself, for the first time realizing what she must look like. She was dressed in shorts and a halter, and her long blond hair was pulled back in a barrette. She wasn't wearing a bit of makeup, and her entire body was coated with a layer of dirt. Beads of sweat were clearly visible on her arms and legs. "I'm a mess."

"Don't worry," Kevin said hurriedly, "I'll get the rest of the weeds later. Did you want to take a shower, Mom?"

She laughed. "Am I that dirty?"

"Not really." Kevin shook his head. "I just thought you might want to get cleaned up before dinner. By the way, what are we having? Something good, I hope."

Delaney frowned at her son. It wasn't like him to be this concerned with propriety. Or to offer her full use of the hot water before he used it all. "I was planning on hot dogs."

Kevin looked disappointed. "Maybe we could order a pizza? I hope you don't mind, but I invited Captain Thomas to stay."

"Oh," Delaney said.

"Hot dogs are fine, Kevin," Lloyd Thomas quickly cut in. A look passed between them, a look Delaney didn't understand and that, deep down, she didn't want to acknowledge.

But Kevin smiled and said, "Great. Hot dogs it is. If you'll excuse me, I'll go light the grill."

When her son hurried toward the patio, Captain Thomas turned to Delaney. "He's a fine boy."

"Yes, he is." Suddenly, she didn't want Captain Lloyd Thomas to stay for dinner. She wanted him to go away and never come back. The man was a threat; she could feel it.

"Shall we?" Lloyd nodded toward the patio.

"Pardon?"

"Maybe we should join Kevin."

"Right." There was nothing to be afraid of, she told herself. She was being foolish. She was acting like a nitwit just because the man was wearing a uniform. Yet she couldn't help being wary. Why was he here? Why was he staying for dinner? But they started walking together. He glanced at her again.

"Kevin tells me your first name is Delaney. That's an unusual name, isn't it?"

"I was named after my mother's side of the family."

"Were they Irish?"

"Right from Dublin."

"May I call you Delaney?"

She shrugged, pausing to put away a shovel. "I suppose."

"Here, I'll get that." He took the shovel from her.

"I'm already dirty," she objected.

But he had slipped the garden tool into its rack inside the shed. "It may not be a gentlemanly thing to say, but you sure *are* dirty," he agreed, smiling at her. He traced a single finger down her nose. "You even have dirt here."

"And you have dirt on your hand now," she pointed out.

"It washes off."

"If it doesn't, you're in big trouble." She indicated his white uniform. "That's parade attire you're wearing, isn't it?"

Lloyd glanced down at his outfit. "The formal name is 'mess dress white,' and yes, I've been to a parade. We had a ceremony out at the naval air station in Glenview."

"Oh. Yes. Glenview." It was only a few miles away. Delaney tried to smile again when she realized he was staring at her differently than before. Or perhaps the look wasn't different, but she had just deciphered it: the look a man gives a woman. His gaze was hot on her body as his narrowed eyes roamed over her intimately, taking in the soft curves of her breasts, the slight swell of her hips. It had been so long since she'd been conscious of a man looking at her that way that she felt her breath quicken in pleasure; at the same time panic crowded her throat.

She started to back away. "Well, if you'll excuse me, maybe I will take that shower."

"Mrs. Anderson," he called, his voice a feather-soft caress. "Delaney."

She turned back to him. "Yes?"

For the longest moment he stared at her as though he wanted to tell her something. Then he said, "Never mind. I'll help Kevin with the grill."

Unfortunately he might help Kevin with more than the grill. He might help Kevin with a military career. That was silly, she told herself. She was imagining things. The man was here because he and her son were friends. He had given Kevin a *ride*. Captains didn't work at recruiting stations.

Not unless they were assigned to a command group, an inner voice nagged.

"I'm sure he'll enjoy the company," she murmured. "If you'll excuse me?"

"Certainly."

Delaney hurried away. When she got to her room and glanced in the mirror she realized that she was absolutely grimy. If Captain Lloyd Thomas had looked at her with anything but distaste, he had to be blind. True, she still had a fairly decent figure, but she wasn't a beauty by any stretch of the imagination. Her hips were too wide and her legs were too long. Although it didn't show, the hair that swept her shoulders was streaked with gray. She could see tiny age lines around her eyes and lips. No one ever seemed surprised to learn that she was the mother of a seventeen-year-old son.

Sighing, she stripped off her shorts and top and headed toward the shower. Captain Lloyd Thomas hadn't given her any look at all, she told herself. The entire episode had to have been wishful thinking on her part.

Yet, she admitted as the hot water streamed over her, even if the look was imaginary, he had certainly awakened some deep stirrings. It had been years since she'd been with a man. At first, when Richard's plane had been shot down and he had been declared missing in action, she had refused to give up hope. She had turned to her three-year-old son, lavishing all her love on Kevin, and for the next seven years she had crusaded with the other wives, trying to uncover news about her husband.

She had been only seventeen when she married Richard. After he disappeared, she got very little financial support from the Navy—just an allotment based on his salary. The only job she could find was as a receptionist in a printing shop. Later, when Richard's body had been found and brought home, she had collected his life insurance. Although that gave her a modest savings, it couldn't cover the cost of an apartment and a car and schooling and all the other expenses that went along with being a parent. And by then she had been so accustomed to living from day to day, intent on raising her child, that she hadn't bothered to change her lifestyle. The few men she had dated hadn't been particularly charmed by a young, exuberant boy and a woman whose conversation centered on *Star Wars* and *The Flintstones*.

As the years passed, she had saved enough money to buy a small house in a good neighborhood in a northwestern suburb of Chicago. When Kevin was old enough to go to school she joined the PTA; when he was a Cub Scout she became a den mother; when he played football she volunteered to be the team mother. She'd sat through rain and snow and bright sunshine, cheering his wins and sharing his losses. She had been so busy being a mother for the past fourteen years that she hadn't had time to be a woman, and suddenly—in the presence of this attractive stranger—she was imagining things.

She shut off the water and reached for a towel. No sense contemplating changes now.

By the time she was ready to go back outside, Delaney had convinced herself that her reaction to Captain Lloyd Thomas had been a mere aberration, the result of a long, hot day. She had also convinced herself that he had given Kevin a ride home simply because he was a nice guy.

"Mmm, smells good," she said, pushing open the screen door and smiling at the two men. They were standing beside the barbecue grill talking, one very blond, the other very dark. Captain Thomas was drinking lemonade. "Don't forget, I like my hot dogs burned."

Kevin smiled back. "Sorry, Mom, you must be smelling the polluted air. We haven't put the hot dogs on yet. We were waiting for you."

"So I get to be chief cook and bottle washer?"

"Just like usual," Kevin said. "Hey, got some go-withs?"

"There's some potato chips in the pantry," she said. "And I have a watermelon in the refrigerator."

"I'll get everything." He seemed glad to rush away.

Delaney picked up the barbecue fork and went to

the grill. "How do you like your hot dogs, Captain Thomas?"

"Lloyd," he corrected. "Burned sounds fine. By the way, you look very pretty."

"Thank you." She had changed into a light sundress and sandals and had piled her hair on top of her head in a loose knot, letting tiny tendrils soften the lines of her face. "Clean at least. Did the dirt come off your hands?"

"It always does."

"Ask a silly question . . ." She smiled. "So where are you stationed, Lloyd? Glenview?"

"Glenview is a naval base," he said after a brief pause.

She frowned. Was he evading the question? "Didn't you say you were there for a parade?"

"Yes."

"And Great Lakes is a naval base, too. You wouldn't be there, would you?"

"Actually I'm not stationed at a military base," he said. "I'm in town with a command group."

"Oh." Delaney turned the hot dogs. That could only mean one thing: He was a recruiter. *No,* her mind screamed, but she forced a bright expression. "How do you like our fair city?"

"It's very nice. Homey."

"Homey? The fastest-growing suburb in the Midwest? You must be from a big city."

"I grew up in rural North Carolina."

"I see." She didn't want to ask, but something drove her. "How long have you known Kevin?"

"We met a few weeks ago."

"At the hardware store?"

There was another brief pause. Finally he said, "I think Kevin should tell you—"

"No, we didn't meet at the hardware store," Kevin interrupted softly, coming back outside.

Delaney turned to glance at her son, her heart thudding with dread. *Don't say it. Please don't say it.*

"I met Captain Thomas at the recruiting station. Mom—" He paused and took a deep breath. "I've joined the Marines."

Delaney stared at her son for a long moment, feeling her hands start to tremble. She clutched the barbecue fork tightly. "Don't joke around, Kevin."

"I'm not joking, Mom."

"Why? Why did you do that?"

"Because I want to be a Marine."

What kind of an answer was that? She tried to stay calm, rational, but she wanted to scream and cry and shake some sense into the boy. "Look, Kevin, you couldn't have joined the Marines. You're only seventeen."

"I'll be eighteen in two months," he answered. "I'd like you to sign the papers so I can be inducted right after graduation."

Delaney looked from her son to Captain Thomas, who stood silently, watching. "Graduation is just two weeks from now," she said.

"Actually, it's ten days," Kevin said. "If you don't sign, I'll go anyhow, after my birthday," he added quietly but firmly. "Either way, I'm joining."

Although her stomach was churning, Delaney smiled brightly. "Well, this certainly isn't the time to discuss it, Kevin. Why don't we talk later? I'm sure

Captain Thomas is hungry, so let's have a pleasant dinner before we go into this."

"We need to talk now, Mom. I don't want to put it off any longer. We've danced around the subject for long enough."

He had been anticipating her reaction. "You can't go, Kevin," Delaney said angrily, dropping all pretense of calm. "I won't let you."

"Mom, I have to do this."

"No, you don't." She turned to Captain Thomas. "Did you put him up to this?"

"Kevin came to me, Mrs. Anderson. I didn't go to him."

So it was Mrs. Anderson now. "But you tempted him. You made it sound wonderful. Look at you. You're all show, with your brass buttons and your white uniform and—and . . ." She couldn't finish. "Why are you here?"

"Because Kevin asked me to come home with him while he broke the news to you. He took the aptitude tests and did very well."

She whirled on her son, trying to hold back the tears that sprang to her eyes. That's where he had been all day, taking tests to become a Marine. "We've made plans, Kevin. You're going to college. You've been accepted at Northwestern."

"Mom, we can't afford Northwestern."

They had already been denied financial aid, because she owned property and had a savings account. "We can get a second mortgage on the house, Kevin."

"I don't want you to do that, Mom. I don't want you to go into debt for me. You've always sacrificed and scrimped and saved for me, and I'm tired of it."

"You can go to the state university," she said. "The University of Illinois is a good school. I can afford it. It can't cost that much."

"Mom, I'm joining the Marines."

"Kevin, please." She swallowed the knot in her throat, trying to hold herself together. "Your father died in the service."

"You've told me that every day of my life, Mom. Grandpa and Uncle Todd were soldiers, and they also died in the service. But Uncle Harry died, too, and he never went near a military base. He choked to death on a roast beef sandwich!"

"Kevin!"

"What's the matter, Mom? That's not a nice thing to say? Look, Uncle Harry is dead. He's just as dead as Dad. Oh, hell!" Suddenly he turned on his heel. "I can't talk about it anymore."

"Kevin!"

But her son just slammed inside the house. A moment later, she heard him leave through the front door, slamming it behind him. He was gone. She was losing her son.

Delaney wasn't aware of Lloyd Thomas taking the barbecue fork from her hand. She wasn't aware of him sitting her down on one of the picnic benches, either, until he spoke. "I hope you like your hot dogs really burned," he said softly, placing the platter on the table and sitting down across from her, "because these are cremated."

She stared at the plate of food. The hot dogs were charred beyond recognition. "I'm not hungry anyway."

"He's grown up, Delaney," Lloyd Thomas went on. "You have to accept that."

"I know," she murmured.

"He knew it was going to be hard for you."

"Is that why he brought you home?"

He nodded. "Yes."

It was illogical, but for some reason she blamed Captain Thomas for Kevin's decision. "I wish I could say thank you, but I can't."

"I understand that."

"Do you?" she said angrily. "Do you know how it feels to lose someone you love to the armed services? Not once, not twice, but three times? To have someone knock on your door and know it's bad news?"

"I've never lost anybody, Delaney, but I understand what you're going through."

"How?" she asked, even angrier. "Tell me how you can understand these things. Do you have a child?"

"Kevin is a man now, Delaney, and there are certain things he has to prove to himself."

"Answer me, dammit!" she nearly shouted. "Do you have children?"

"No," he said quietly, "I don't have children."

"Then how can you know how I feel? How can you say you understand? You don't understand any of it. You never worried when he was little and had a fever. You never nursed him through chicken pox. You never sat up until dawn because he had the car and it was prom night." She tried to choke back tears, but they were streaming down her face by now. "You're taking him away from me. You're taking my son."

"I'm not taking him away from you, Delaney—"

"The military, then," she interrupted snidely. "The *Marines* are taking him." She spat out the word.

"The wonderful Marine Corps—pride, tradition, spirit. Being a Marine is the only thing that counts."

"Kevin is leaving of his own volition." As he spoke, Lloyd handed her his handkerchief. "He's growing up and there's nothing you can do to prevent that, Delaney."

She took the handkerchief from him and sat still for a moment, clutching it in her hands. "I love him," she whispered at last. "I can't let him go."

"If you love him, you have to let him go," Lloyd said softly. "You have to let him be his own person."

"I can't protect him in the Marines."

"He doesn't need your protection any longer, Delaney. He needs your support and your love, but this is something he has to do for himself."

Delaney stared at her hands, not really seeing them as she twisted the handkerchief around and around. She knew he was right. She had to let go, but it wasn't easy. For seventeen years she had loved and protected Kevin; she'd been essentially alone all that time, a single parent trying to raise a child all by herself.

"How long have you been a widow?" he asked.

At first she couldn't answer. She didn't want to think about anything except Kevin. Then she sighed, "Forever." She glanced up at him. "Richard's plane was shot down when Kevin was three years old."

"Air Force?"

"Navy. When I met him he was stationed at Great Lakes. We got married as soon as he finished boot camp. We had two weeks together before he shipped out to the Mediterranean."

"You've lived alone all these years?"

"Yes."

"Where are your folks?"

Why was she telling him all this? He was a total stranger. Yet, despite her resentment—and her outburst—she felt his sympathy. "Florida. After my father was killed, my mother remarried. My stepfather likes warm climates."

"So you were really alone. That had to be tough." He paused. "You know Kevin is planning to go to college after his stint in the Marine Corps. We'll educate him."

She didn't want to say it, but the thought haunted her. "If he lives."

"Delaney, you can't dwell on the fact that he might die."

"Why not? I've lost three people to the military. Why should I expect anything else?"

"You know that's unusual."

"But it still happened. They're still dead."

"And as Kevin pointed out, a person can die while crossing the street."

"I suppose." Delaney sighed again. "That kind of death just doesn't seem to hurt as much."

"I think it does hurt as much, Delaney. It's just not as dramatic. When Kevin comes back, he'll need your support."

"I know."

"Then you'll sign the papers?"

She could refuse to grant him permission. She could spend the next two months trying to talk her son out of joining the Marines. But in her heart she knew objecting would be futile. Arguing with him would just create more animosity, and eventually it would drive them apart. After his birthday, Kevin would be able to enlist without her consent. "I don't have much choice, do I?" she said. "If I don't sign, he'll go anyway."

"I guess you would just be postponing the inevitable."

"He's always been so stubborn, so determined. Even when he was a little boy he had to do everything himself—his way."

"You have a right to be proud of him."

"I am proud of him. I guess that's what hurts so much, because in many ways I can understand why he's doing this." She blew her nose and glanced at Lloyd. For someone so tough, so strong, the man seemed strangely tender. The combination confused her. "I've really made a fool of myself with all this blubbering."

"No more than anyone else would have in the same circumstances."

"Do you do this often?"

"No. But Kevin was worried about you. You know, he thinks you're very special, too."

"Does he?" That was nice to hear.

"And now that I've met you, I can understand why."

She smiled wryly. "I was covered with dirt when you met me, and all I've done since then is cry. You call that special?"

"I call it very special." He smiled and reached for his hat. "And on that note I'd better be going. You'll want to be alone with Kevin when he comes back. Will you be all right now?"

She doubted she would ever be all right again, but she could hardly burden this stranger any more than she already had. She nodded. "Thanks for the shoulder."

"Any time." He smiled again, but his expression was as bittersweet as she felt. He started to leave, then turned back. "Delaney," he said softly, "I'm sorry."

For some reason she could tell that he meant it. He was truly sorry. "Thank you."

"I'm not the enemy, you know."

She studied him for a long moment. He was standing there in his white uniform, hat in hand. A soldier. Everybody's hero. And suddenly fear and anguish squeezed her throat so tightly that she could hardly breathe. "No," she said at last, "you're not the enemy. But don't you see . . . you're worse than the enemy. In Kevin's eyes you're some kind of hero, and I can't compete with that."

Chapter 2

THE NEXT TEN days passed swiftly and—for Delaney—fruitlessly. Despite her decision not to fight Kevin, she couldn't resist trying to talk him out of joining the Marines. At every opportunity, she showed him college brochures, pointed out other things he could do instead. But no matter what she said, her son was adamant.

The morning Kevin left home she went to work, as usual. She thought about calling in sick, but since he had left at the crack of dawn there didn't seem to be much else to do—except sit at home and sob her heart out.

Years ago Delaney had thought about going back to school, but there never seemed to be enough time.

And something always happened that required her to spend the tuition money she had saved. Either the furnace needed repair or the muffler fell off her car or Kevin needed a new jacket. Unable to further her education Delaney had stayed at the same print shop for fourteen years.

She greeted customers and filled out forms all morning as if in a fog, wondering the entire time where Kevin was, what he was doing, whether he was all right. She kept thinking that he might die, and that she couldn't protect him. By the time the print shop was ready to close, Delaney was emotionally as well as physically exhausted—and she was totally unprepared for the sight of Lloyd Thomas.

She looked up automatically when the door opened. He stepped inside the shop, and oddly, her heart skipped a beat. She hadn't seen him since the day Kevin had made his announcement, and she was amazed to see him now. He was wearing dress blues this time. He looked so formal, so handsome, yet for a moment all she could feel was resentment. Was he here to remind her that she'd just lost her son to the Marines?

"Oo-la-la," the other receptionist murmured, scraping her chair back to stand up. "Check out the guy in uniform. Where's our flag? I could get real patriotic with somebody that good-looking."

Jean was happily married, but she was always joking about men. Unfortunately Delaney wasn't in the mood for jokes today. "I'll help him," she said, standing up.

Jean glanced at Delaney with pretended astonishment. "What?"

"I'll *help* him," Delaney repeated.

The other woman grinned. "Since when do you leap up at the sight of a handsome man?"

"It's not like that," Delaney said. "I know him."

"Oh." Jean's grin broadened. "Lucky you."

Delaney went to the counter. "Captain Thomas," she said, unable to hide either her surprise or her resentment. "What can I do for you?"

"Lloyd," he corrected, smiling at her. "How've you been?"

But Delaney didn't smile back; she couldn't. "Fine."

"Good. Glad to hear it." He held up several sheets of typing paper, clearly sensing her mood but not acknowledging it. "I have some important letters to write, and I remember Kevin mentioning that you worked here. I wondered if you could make me up some stationery."

Delaney wasn't mollified that easily. "Did you come here to gloat?"

He looked at her, his eyes steady and unapologetic. "I came for stationery."

"Doesn't the government provide you with stationery?"

"Not personalized."

She sighed, suddenly ashamed. It wasn't this man's fault that Kevin had joined the Marines. "I'm sorry. I shouldn't have struck out at you. I'm feeling blue today."

"I know," he answered softly. "I thought you might be. And actually, I didn't come in just for stationery. I came to tell you that Kevin's fine."

"You've heard from him?" Delaney couldn't keep the excitement from her voice.

"Not from Kevin himself," Lloyd said, "but I

called Parris Island this afternoon and I understand he's settling in well."

"Thank you," she murmured. Her son had left the house at four o'clock that morning to catch a bus to O'Hare Airport. From there he and several other recruits were scheduled to fly to the training base at Parris Island, South Carolina. "I was worried about him."

"I hear the haircut is over with and they've had their first meal."

"You mean the Marines still shave the recruits' heads?"

He laughed. "That's one tradition that I don't think will ever end. I'm afraid Kevin is as good as bald right now."

She laughed, too. "When he was little he once told the barber to shave his head. He looked awful."

"It'll grow back."

"True." Deeply embarrassed at the way she had treated Lloyd, Delaney tried to smile. "Thanks again. I appreciate your coming here. It's really nice of you."

"I'm a nice guy," he said.

"Contrary to the opinion of most mothers?" Delaney added.

He laughed again. "Unfortunately."

"Now I'm doubly ashamed."

"Ashamed enough to go out to dinner with me tonight?" he asked quickly. "There's a great restaurant a few blocks from here that I've been wanting to try."

He was trying to make her feel better. Delaney smiled again, but shook her head. "I don't think I'd be very pleasant company tonight."

Lloyd shrugged. "I'm willing to take that risk."

She stared at him for a long moment. She could hear Jean shuffling papers in the background, but Delaney knew her friend was just trying to look busy while she was shamelessly eavesdropping on the conversation. "I don't know, Lloyd. I don't think—"

"I hear this place has the best cheesecake in the northwest suburbs," he cut in smoothly.

How did he know she liked cheesecake?

"Just imagine it," he went on. "Rich, firm cheesecake piled high with juicy strawberries."

She couldn't help smiling. "Zap, right to the hips," she said, blurting out the first thing that came to mind. "And mine are already too wide."

He frowned and tilted his head to assess her backside critically. "Maybe just a tad."

"Gee, thanks," she said, but she wasn't angry. What had she expected? It had been a long time since she'd talked to a man this way. She'd almost forgotten the rules.

"Sorry." He grinned, a charming lopsided smile. "I didn't mean that as an insult. You have nice hips."

"Really?" The man went from bad to worse.

Apparently he thought so too, for he laughed and said, "I think I better quit now while I only have one foot in my mouth. So what do you say? Feel like having some cheesecake?"

She didn't want to burden him with her troubles, but suddenly, she didn't want to be alone either. She glanced back at Jean who was grinning smugly. Delaney turned to Lloyd. "Cheesecake sounds great."

"Good." He sounded surprised. "What time do you get off?"

She glanced at the wall clock. "We're officially closed in ten seconds."

"Do you want me to wait outside?"

"You can wait here. I'll be just a minute." When she went back to her desk, she saw that Jean's grin still hadn't diminished. "Wow," she whispered. "The man is awesome, Delaney. Where did you meet him?"

"Something must be wrong with your reasoning powers, Jean," Delaney whispered back. "If you'd been listening closely, you could have figured out that Kevin introduced me to him."

Jean's smile faded instantly, and the woman looked stricken. "Oh, Lord, Delaney, I'm sorry. I should have known. He's Kevin's draft officer?"

There was no such thing as a draft officer, but Delaney didn't feel like going into a long explanation. "Sort of. He's the Marine recruiter."

Jean glanced at Lloyd again. "No wonder they're only looking for a few good men. There aren't many guys who could measure up to those standards."

In spite of her gloomy mood, Delaney heard herself laugh. "You've been watching too much television, my friend," she said. "That commercial doesn't have anything to do with looks."

Jean shrugged. "You interpret the advertising slogan your way and I'll interpret it my way. The man is a hunk." She grinned. "Have fun. Don't eat too much."

"I won't."

When Delaney turned back to Lloyd she saw him with new eyes. Before, when he'd come to her house, she had thought he was attractive. Suddenly she realized how truly good-looking he was. He stood near the door, talking to Martin, one of the printers, and his mere presence seemed to dwarf the room. His royal and dark blue uniform fit perfectly, stretching across broad shoulders, tapering to a taut waist and narrow hips. He must have just been somewhere important. She knew from her days as a military brat that although less formal than mess whites, dress blues were reserved for special affairs.

Sensing that she was staring at him, Lloyd turned to her and smiled. "Ready?"

Delaney caught herself. The man was attractive, all right, but the last thing she needed was to get involved with a Marine. Quickly she pulled her sweater around her shoulders. "Yes, I'm ready."

"'Night," Martin called as Lloyd placed his hand at the small of her back, steering her toward the door.

"See you in the morning," Delaney answered, glancing back just in time to see Jean give her a thumbs-up sign.

"Make every moment count," the other woman called, winking.

Delaney looked at Lloyd, wondering if he had heard Jean's remark, but he seemed preoccupied. They walked across the parking lot. Suddenly, she noticed her car and realized that in her confusion she hadn't considered what she would do with it.

"Maybe you'd better give me directions to the restaurant. I—I could meet you there," she said hesitantly. Perhaps she shouldn't go, after all. She didn't really want to be with anyone tonight, let alone *this* man, who had taken her son away.

"Nonsense," Lloyd said, opening the door of his white and red Chevrolet El Camino. "I'll bring you back here afterward. It's silly to waste gas."

"I suppose." Delaney shrugged. She didn't want to make a scene. Yet she was vividly aware of Lloyd in the close confines of the car. He seemed bigger than ever, and more of a threat.

"We forgot to choose your stationery," she said after a long moment.

He gave her a quick grin. "There's always tomorrow."

They arrived at the restaurant a few moments later. The place was crowded, but the hostess seated them right away. As they entered, every woman turned and stared, including the waitress, who smiled at Lloyd in blatant invitation. Delaney slid into the booth, and Lloyd sat across from her, placing his hat to one side. Even when he relaxed, his movements were precise, soldierlike.

"Am I that intimidating?" he said after the attractive waitress had taken their orders and sauntered off.

"Pardon?"

"Most mothers seem to like me well enough, but you're so quiet that I'm beginning to think you're afraid of me."

"I don't know what to talk to you about," she said honestly. "Unless you watch cartoons?"

He laughed. "You mean Kevin hasn't outgrown cartoons yet?"

"Yes, I guess he has." She smiled, remembering. "But I've memorized half of the plots. I used to watch them with him all the time."

"Until the cartoons turned into island movies with Brooke Shields running around half naked?"

"Yes." She glanced at him, surprised. "How did you know?"

"Island movies with naked women are an important part of the rites of manhood."

"I suppose," she agreed. Since that subject now seemed to be exhausted, Delaney set out to learn more about the man who'd lured her son into the military. "How long have you been a Marine?" she asked.

"Nineteen years."

"One more year until retirement."

He nodded. "I may stay in a bit longer."

So he was a rah-rah boy, all enthusiasm. Of course, he would have to be enthusiastic to be a recruiter. "Do you like the Marines that much?"

"Yes, I do. Does that surprise you?" He met her gaze. "You know, Delaney, the military's a good place for a person without attachments."

Delaney certainly couldn't argue that point. She objected to what it did to people *with* attachments. "You don't have any family?"

"My folks are still in North Carolina," he said. "My ex-wife lives there, too, but I'm more or less alone."

She was surprised to hear that he had been married; somehow Lloyd struck her as a bachelor. "I remember you mentioned you didn't have any children."

"Yes. In a way I'm glad. At least some poor innocent kid didn't have to suffer through the mess."

Delaney raised her eyebrows. "Was your divorce very sticky?"

"My *marriage* was sticky," he said. "Unfortunately Amy just wasn't stable enough to cope with military life. She couldn't stand those long stretches when I had to be away."

"Women seldom are equipped to deal with the loneliness."

He looked at her for a long moment. Once again Delaney sensed his empathy. "Were you lonely?"

"Yes," she answered honestly, "I was very lonely. But at least I had Kevin."

Lloyd nodded. "I know what you mean. I work with some youth groups in the area, and I've really appreciated getting to know some of the boys. Especially Curt."

"He's one you're especially close to?"

"Yes, I've been helping Curt—or at least I hope I'm helping him," he amended. "Speaking of kids," he went on, "I understand from Kevin that your father was career Army."

Delaney was amazed at how much Lloyd knew about her. She was curious about him, too. At times he sounded lonely himself, and vulnerable. Did he need somebody, too? "My father was about as career as a person can get," she answered. "He loved the Army."

"How did he die?"

It had been over twenty years since her father died, and Delaney no longer cried when she thought of him. "On a peacekeeping mission in the Far East."

"And your uncle Todd?"

"He was Army too—infantry. He was assigned to a base in Germany. One day during combat practice he stepped on an old land mine no one knew about." Delaney looked down at her place setting.

Lloyd shook his head. "Left over from the war. That's rough."

"Yes, it was very hard on us all, especially my aunt." Why was she trying to provoke Lloyd? Delaney knew she sounded argumentative, but she couldn't seem to silence her anger and bitterness.

Lloyd studied her for a long moment. "Did your aunt know what she was getting into when she fell in love with him?"

"I don't think that's the point, is it?"

"There are a lot of dangerous jobs in this world, Delaney," he said, slowly twirling his water glass. "The military doesn't have a patent on risk. Besides, women have been worrying about men since time began. I think it's a given."

"And therefore acceptable?"

"I didn't say that," he retorted. "You did."

"Pain is a fact of life, too, but that doesn't make it good."

"True," he agreed. "I don't want to suffer any more than the next guy. Hell, I don't want to suffer at all, but sometimes a person has to bleed."

"And take risks?"

"Yes," he said firmly, "and take risks. There aren't any guarantees."

She sighed. "Unfortunately." In her heart she knew he was right; she just didn't like having to admit it. And this was a bad day. "I'm sorry, Lloyd. I seem to be striking out at you again."

A slow, understanding smile lit his face. "I'll remember to wear my armor next time."

Would there be a next time? "I'm in a foul mood," she said. "And I feel very hostile toward the military. It's taken so much away from me—my father, my uncle, my husband . . . and now my son."

"No one's denying your right to be upset, Delaney."

She stared at him for a moment. "Yet a person has to take the bad with the good?"

"You could put it that way," he said.

She smiled. "Okay. Let's change the subject. How do you feel about the local election campaigns? Do you think the stumping is starting too early?"

"Politics? Isn't that subject just as dangerous as the last one?"

"It always seems safe to me."

"That's probably because you only talk to fellow Republicans," he said, winking at her. "I'm a Democrat."

She blinked in astonishment. He knew she was a Republican? "It seems Kevin told you a lot about me."

"Just the things he thought might be significant," Lloyd replied. "I'd like to know more . . . a lot more."

For a moment his soft words caught Delaney off guard. She simply stared at him. Was he really interested in her? The waitress came just then with their food, flirting enthusiastically with Lloyd as she set down their plates. Delaney watched the young woman, realizing that she no longer even knew how to flirt.

When the girl had gone, Lloyd leaned toward Delaney. "Something wrong?"

"She's very pretty," Delaney said, nodding at the waitress.

"Yes, she is," he agreed. "But so are you."

"You must be a fellow Irishman, Captain Thomas."

He looked puzzled. "Actually my mother is Greek

and my father is German. Why would you think I'm Irish?"

"Because you seem to have kissed the Blarney stone."

To her surprise Lloyd didn't laugh. "You're not very good at accepting compliments, are you, Delaney?"

The last male who complimented her had been one of Kevin's teammates: He'd told her she made a mean chocolate chip cookie. "No, I guess I'm not," she admitted. "I'm sorry."

"You apologize too much, too."

"Then I'm not sorry."

"Which is probably closer to the truth." Lloyd laughed and nodded toward their food. "How about a real truce? Let's eat."

For the rest of the meal they talked about trivial things—the salad dressing, sports, the weather. They ate cheesecake loaded with strawberries for dessert. Delaney found she was enjoying herself; she was certainly becoming aware of Lloyd Thomas as a man.

Now that she had taken the time to study him, she could understand why the waitress had flirted with him. There was something exciting about him, like electricity in the air, and it wasn't just his physical appearance. She watched as he wrapped his hands around his coffee cup as if to warm them. The blue of his eyes was almost startling.

"Do I pass?" he said suddenly, breaking her concentration.

She blinked, trying to grasp his meaning. "What?"

"Inspection," he clarified. "You were staring at

me. For a moment I thought maybe you were trying to choose the best way to get back at me."

"I was looking at the branch insignia on your collar." She could hardly admit that she had been daydreaming about him. "They're interesting." They were silver and gold, a globe with an eagle on top and an anchor.

"You've never seen the Marine emblem before?"

"No; my father was Army and my husband was Navy."

"Oh. Right," he said.

Glancing at him, Delaney realized he cared as little about the symbols as she did. And she hadn't fooled him—he knew exactly what she had been looking at—and why.

He picked up his hat and nodded at her empty plate. "Finished?"

"Yes." She gathered her sweater and purse and slid out of the booth.

Lloyd guided her to the front of the restaurant. Once again Delaney noticed heads turning as they passed. When Lloyd paused to pay the bill she couldn't help noticing that the waitress slipped a piece of paper in his hand.

"What if you were married?" Delaney said as they walked out into the parking lot. It was dark outside, and she realized that they had been in the restaurant for quite some time.

Lloyd smiled. "You saw the waitress give me her phone number?"

"She wasn't very subtle about it."

"I guess I'll throw it away."

This time she smiled. "Sure."

Lloyd opened the car door for her. "You don't believe me?"

"No," she said. After he had gotten in on his side she asked, "Are women often attracted by your uniform?"

He started the car, a frown marring his forehead. "Delaney, I wouldn't dare answer that question. Either way, I'd be sure to incriminate myself."

She laughed. "I suppose so."

They lapsed into a comfortable silence. Delaney leaned back against the seat enjoying the soft breeze that blew in the open window, feathering her hair away from her cheeks. The night was beautiful, clear and perfect, with a few stars overhead sparkling like tiny diamonds. It seemed unfair that the night could be so lovely when she felt so miserable. Suddenly she realized it had been several hours since she had so much as thought about Kevin. She felt like a traitor.

"Something wrong?" Lloyd asked.

She turned to him in surprise. "I was just thinking about Kevin."

"He's probably in bed right now, asleep."

"This early?"

"Boot camp is rough. He'll be exhausted every night by the time he gets back to the barracks."

"True," she agreed, remembering the movies she'd seen about boot camp. "I hear Parris Island is the roughest."

Lloyd didn't confirm or deny her claim. He merely said, "We do pride ourselves on discipline and hard work."

She glanced at Lloyd in the darkness of the car. Captain Lloyd Thomas was strong; he had character.

She could see it in the lines of his face, in his arms, in his hands as they gripped the steering wheel.

When Lloyd passed the turnoff that would have taken them back to the print shop, where her car was parked, her attention returned to the road. "Where are you going?"

"I thought we'd go for a ride. Do you mind?"

She glanced at her watch. "It's kind of late."

"How old are you, Delaney?"

She felt herself blush. "Why?"

"You don't *look* old enough to fall asleep at nine o'clock."

"You mean I act like an old lady," she said. "I guess I do. I'm so accustomed to being home at a certain time, to be sure I'm there when Kevin comes in." But Kevin was gone. "I guess I've gotten into a rut."

"It's called motherhood. But there's hope for you."

She looked at him again. "You're sure?"

"I'm positive," he said solemnly. It seemed natural for him to take her hand. But there was absolutely no reason for her pulse to hop and skip all over the place. "All you have to do is learn how to be yourself again, instead of just Kevin's mother."

"Are you saying mothers aren't individuals?"

He glanced at her as he drove into a forest preserve and pulled up alongside a row of parked cars. "I think that's another one I'd better back away from."

"I'll let you off the hook this time." Delaney looked at the other cars parked in the darkness. "Where are we?"

"It's a lovers' lane."

For a moment Delaney couldn't believe her ears. *Lovers' lane?* Anger flared inside her, hot and quick, and she pulled her hand away from his. "You're one smooth operator, Lloyd. Did you really think you could score with me this easily? Comforting the distraught mother. That's as bad as preying on widows."

"Score with you?" he repeated. "Delaney, do you think I brought you here to neck?"

At least the car was dark, and he couldn't see her blush. "I *know* you did."

"Delaney, come off it." He actually tossed his head back and laughed.

"I fail to see the humor in this," she said testily. The man had a lot of nerve.

He laughed again. Then he sobered and said, "Delaney, if I wanted to neck with you, I'd know better than to bring you to a lovers' lane."

She knew it was silly and unreasonable but for some reason his rejection cut through her like a splinter of ice. She clamped her lips together to keep from snapping at him.

"Now you're angry with me." He shook his head. "But I can see how this must look to you, and I'm sorry I offended you." Sighing, he went on, "Delaney, we're two mature people. I'll admit that I would like to kiss you. I find you very attractive. But I wouldn't bring you to a lovers' lane because you're not the type." He paused. "Neither am I." Opening the car door, he tugged her hand. "Now. Come on. I want to show you something."

She felt foolish; she didn't want to get involved with him. Lloyd was a Marine—the enemy. And he had just admitted that he found her attractive. She was so vulnerable now; she should get right back in

the car and have him take her to the print shop. She
should run the other way.

"Delaney?"

It was crazy, but she took his hand.

They walked along the path that bordered the
small lake. For the longest time neither of them
spoke. In the distance Delaney could hear insects
calling, the occasional croak of a bullfrog. Now and
then a ripple broke the smooth surface of the water,
illuminated by the moon. A beaver splashed near the
shore.

After a while, Lloyd sat on a bench overlooking a
stream that fed the lake, and pulled her down beside
him. "Look." He indicated another beaver dam a few
yards downstream.

"They're industrious, aren't they?" Delaney remarked.

"Yes, they are," he answered. "Those are the offspring of this pair."

She knew what he was getting at. "And they do
very well without their mother?"

"Yes, because they've been well trained," he said.
"Before the young can survive on their own, the parents have to teach them certain skills."

"It's a cold, cruel world, even for beavers?" she
said dryly. "I admire your intention, Lloyd, but your
logic is skewed. You can't equate these animals with
people. I'm upset about Kevin joining the Marines. I
always will be, and all the beaver offspring in the
world, no matter how independent they are, won't
change my mind."

"I don't want to change your mind, Delaney," he
said. "I know I can't. All I want to do is help you

accept what's happened. There are some things you don't have any control over."

"But the pain's still there, Lloyd. I may not want it, but it's there. Some things are inevitable."

She hadn't realized she was crying until he brushed a tear from her cheek, his callused thumb rough against her soft skin. The gesture was so tender that she felt her throat constrict with a strange new emotion.

"Don't cry," he said softly. "Please don't cry."

"I can't help it."

"I know." As they sat there in the moonlight he rubbed his thumb back and forth across her cheek. Then suddenly he lowered his head to hers. "And I can't help it, either," he went on huskily. "You're right, Delaney. Some things are inevitable."

And then his lips met hers.

Chapter 3

AT FIRST HIS lips were soft on hers. For a moment Delaney felt as though they were alone in the universe, in the vast darkness of space. She felt dizzy, as though she were whirling through the atmosphere. Stars exploded in her head; brilliant supernovas burst open in a kaleidoscope of colors, and a white-hot flame swept through her.

"Delaney," Lloyd murmured against her mouth. "My sweet Delaney."

Suddenly she was crushed against him, and the heat intensified, blazing in a feverish thrill as he moved his lips commandingly over hers. Unconsciously she arched against him as long-repressed emotions—need, longing, desire—clamored for release. She felt as if a whirlwind had been unleashed inside her and was raging uncontrolled. Everywhere he touched was quickly inflamed; the heat of his hands burned through the thin fabric of her dress, branding her.

Lloyd was the one to pull away. Drawing a ragged breath, he placed his hands on her shoulders and stepped back. "My Lord, Delaney," he whispered hoarsely. "I'm sorry. I didn't mean for that to happen."

Delaney could hardly form coherent thoughts, let alone speak. "My," she murmured, "we seem to be apologizing a lot, don't we?"

"We do seem to be up on all the social amenities." He traced his thumb over her lips. They felt swollen where he had kissed her. "I'm sorry. You're welcome. Thank you."

"All but good night," she added, trying to gather her wits together. She wanted to throw herself into his arms and beg him to kiss her again, and for a moment she felt herself sway toward him. She tried to focus on her watch. "Speaking of which, it's late. I have to work tomorrow."

"So do I," he said. "Perhaps we should get back."

She walked beside him to the car, wondering what to say. She felt so awkward, like a silly teenager, which was ridiculous—all they had done was to kiss.

Oh, but what a kiss. Even now the intensity of it frightened her. It had been years since she had been kissed by a man and she didn't have much basis for comparison; still, she knew without a doubt that never, *never* in her life had she experienced an embrace quite like that. His lips had felt so sensuous, his body rock-hard against hers, and she had responded wholeheartedly. Whatever was the matter with her? She'd just sent her son off to the service this morning and by nightfall she was falling into the enemy's arms.

Lloyd didn't say anything as they walked to his car. He opened the door, helped her inside, and went around to slip behind the wheel. Delaney stared out the window as he started the engine. Cars were parked on either side of them, their windows all steamed up.

Lloyd finally broke the silence.

"Do you like the outdoors?"

"I'm not a typical Ivory girl, but I like the grass and trees. Why?"

He shrugged. "Have you ever walked in the rain?"

"Not by choice."

"Ever gone swimming by moonlight?"

"No. Have you?"

"Yes."

She shook her head. "I'm usually too tired to do anything by moonlight except sleep."

"You need to start living again, Delaney."

She glanced at him, sharply this time. "I never stopped living."

"You're so solemn," he said, looking at her curiously. "Were you always so serious, even as a young girl?"

She frowned, trying to remember. She knew she had been more carefree as a girl, but those days seemed so long ago. She had married young, throwing caution to the wind, and she had given birth to Kevin when she was just seventeen. "No."

"What made you so solemn?"

She shrugged. "Life, I suppose." *The military.*

But she didn't say that. And in her heart she knew the military wasn't entirely to blame. Motherhood had changed her. The day Kevin was born she had felt overwhelmed by responsibility. From that moment on, she had taken her role in life very seriously indeed, and when Richard died, she had faced the future with bleak determination rather than hopeful anticipation. Even if her husband had lived, she would have felt the same sense of responsibility toward her son. Delaney knew she had shut out the men who had tried to get close to her over the years; she'd been too busy being a mother.

"Life's to blame?" he repeated, bringing her back to the present. "You have a pretty grim outlook, Delaney."

She shrugged again. "I suppose you think life is a ball?"

He shot her a quick glance. "I don't seem to be saying the right things tonight, do I?"

She sighed in self-disgust. It wasn't like her to be so testy. "Why don't we both lighten up, Lloyd? I'm in a blue funk because I've lost my son. And you're not exactly cheerful, either. It must be the full moon."

"Experts have disputed that theory," he said. "They say people's behavior has nothing to do with the phases of the moon. Of course, the same experts say there's no man in the moon, either."

She glanced up at the silvery ball in the sky, then looked at Lloyd. *"No* one really believes that."

"Since you're the serious type, you certainly wouldn't," he pointed out.

"And you do, I suppose," she said wryly. "Come on, Lloyd. Stop putting me on!"

He laughed and then turned serious again. "I believe that men and women have the ability to accomplish anything they set out to do. In other words, I believe everyone should have a dream, and enough courage to go for it."

"An admirable attitude." She kept her voice light. No need to let him know that she envied his optimism.

A moment later, he pulled into the print shop's parking lot. She started to open her car door. "Thank you for dinner."

Lloyd got out of the car and walked around to open her door. "I'll follow you home."

"Don't be silly—"

"I'm not being silly," he interrupted, taking her firmly by the hand. "It's called being polite. So don't bother to argue."

She didn't. All of a sudden she was much too tired. Her car was alone in the lot, a banged-up blue Pinto.

Delaney found her keys and turned to thank him again. It was a mistake for they were very close together, and it seemed the most natural thing in the world for him to kiss her. She felt drawn to him like the tide pulled to shore by the moon.

His lips were soft, and he held her close. As if by magic her arms went around his neck, and she entwined her fingers in his dark hair. The elegant gold buttons on his uniform jacket pressed into her, but she was hardly aware of the sensation, concentrating only on the feel of his mouth against hers, the leanness of his body, the strength of his arms.

The kiss ended all too soon. Once again he drew away. "Good night, Delaney," he murmured huskily.

"Good night." She dropped her arms and turned to her car. Without understanding how she could accomplish it, she got inside and rolled down the window.

Lloyd leaned on the frame. "Drive carefully," he said. "I'll call you tomorrow."

No! she wanted to shout. Please don't call me. My defenses are down and I'm too vulnerable. When you kiss me I go limp. Instead she said, "I have to mow the lawn tomorrow after work."

"Didn't Kevin do that before he left?"

"He was too busy getting ready to leave."

"How about the next day?"

What could she say? "I have to finish up some chores around the house."

"Saturday?"

"I'm—"

"Working," he cut in. "Never mind. I'll see you soon. Okay?"

"Sure." She nodded, still light-headed from his kiss. Was he really backing off, giving her some time? Thank goodness. She knew she couldn't resist him for very long. "Well, good night again."

"'Night," he said. As usual the engine was slow to catch, and Delaney ground the starter.

"Sounds like you need a tune-up."

For a moment she blushed furiously; then she realized he was talking about the car. Good lord! What was happening? She couldn't even think straight. "What I need is a new car," she murmured.

And now that Kevin had joined the Marines instead of going to college, she could probably afford one.

"I don't know." He studied the beat-up Pinto. "I think the old girl has character."

This old girl has character, too, Delaney thought, and enough sense to get the hell out of here. If only she could start the car. At last the engine roared to life.

"It just has a lot of dents," she said. By then she had managed to collect herself. She shifted the car into gear. "Thanks for everything."

"You're welcome. Drive carefully, Delaney. I'll be right behind you."

She didn't bother to object; it probably wouldn't do any good. The only thing that would do her any good would be to get home as quickly as possible. She could feel her defenses crumbling slowly, brick by brick, and she'd only spent five hours with the man.

Delaney didn't give Lloyd a chance to walk her to her door. That might have meant another kiss. Instead she pulled into her driveway, parked, and practically ran up the walk, waving as she inserted the key in the front door.

He waved back and drove away.

Sighing with relief, Delaney closed the door and leaned against it. Lord, she was tired.

She headed for the bedroom, pulling off her clothes as she went and letting them drop in a silky trail. She'd pick them up tomorrow. At least she wasn't going to have any trouble sleeping tonight.

The moment Delaney walked into the print shop the next day, Jean practically pounced on her.

"Okay, Delaney," she said. "What does steel feel like?"

Delaney pretended not to understand. They had worked together for over ten years and knew each other's secrets, but she wasn't ready to share this one yet. It was still too tenuous, too fragile. "Steel?"

"You know that commercial advertising the Marines," Jean explained. "They take steel and form it into a sword."

Delaney scowled. "You should switch to cable."

Now Jean looked puzzled. "Are you saying he didn't do anything?"

"He bought me dinner."

"Dinner?" Jean repeated, snorting in disgust. "Dinner? All that virility in one gorgeous hunk and he bought you dinner? What is he, dead?"

Delaney laughed. "I don't think so."

"But you don't know for sure?"

"Lloyd isn't dead," Delaney said.

"How do you know?"

Delaney sighed. Apparently Jean expected a full explanation. "Take my word for it."

"Hah!" Jean said. "When it comes to men, your word doesn't count."

"What do you mean by that?"

"Oh, Delaney, come on. You know exactly what I mean. You're the proverbial hand that rocks the cradle. You've been so busy being a mother that you wouldn't know what to do with a good-looking man if you tripped over him." She paused, apparently hoping for a response, but when Delaney refused to rise to the bait, Jean gave up and changed the subject. "By the way, have you heard from Kevin?"

Delaney welcomed the new subject. "I understand he's settling in fine."

"Good. Adrienne wants his address. You know, I think my daughter has a crush on your son. Maybe when he comes home on leave, they'll get together."

Delaney was about to tell her that Kevin had had a crush on Adrienne for several years when a customer walked in, cutting their conversation short. Delaney was relieved; this morning she wasn't in the mood for a personal discussion.

The day passed quickly. Every time the door opened, she half expected to see Lloyd striding into the shop. He still needed stationery. While part of her wished he wouldn't, another part of her wanted him to come. Her heart skipped a beat each time a man entered.

The later it got the more disappointed she felt. At six o'clock she left with Jean and Martin.

"Want to come over for dinner?" Jean asked. "We're having liver."

Delaney made a face. "No, thanks."

"What's the matter with liver?"

"Nothing," she said. "Except most people don't like it. See you tomorrow."

"Will you be all right?"

Delaney smiled. "I'll be fine."

"You won't fret about Kevin?"

"I'm going to mow the lawn. That should keep my mind off my son."

"Ugh," Jean declared. "In your place, I'd opt for the liver."

Delaney just waved good-bye. She was pleased when her Pinto started quickly. Perhaps it would run for a few more miles, after all. She was nearly home when a metal part of some sort worked itself loose from underneath the car. It scraped the pavement, making a horrible rattling noise for the next two blocks. By the time she pulled into her driveway the part was so loose that it sounded like someone was beating against a tin drum. Two teenage girls from her neighborhood turned to stare.

Delaney stared back in surprise. The girls were standing in her front yard chatting with Lloyd Thomas, who was busy mowing her lawn. He was dressed in well-worn jeans that rode low on his hips and clung to his thighs. An orange T-shirt with the initials USMC emblazoned across the front stretched tautly across his broad chest. Apparently he enjoyed advertising the Marine Corps during his free time as well.

"Hi, Mrs. Anderson. Sounds pretty bad," one of them called, gesturing toward her car.

Climbing out, Delaney nodded. "Yes, it does."

"Captain Thomas was just telling us how Kevin's doing," the other girl piped in. "We stopped by to get his address."

"Oh," Delaney said. They were wearing too much makeup, but they looked to be all of fourteen. One girl had dyed her hair pink, and it looked as though it had just come out of a waffle iron. How well did Kevin even know them?

"We want to write him a letter."

"If you're too busy to give us his address right now," the first girl said quickly, smiling at Lloyd, "we'd be glad to come back another time."

Delaney smiled, too. "I'll bet."

"Pardon?" the girl said.

Lloyd shut off the lawn mower and strode toward

her. Delaney took a deep breath. One look at him was almost more than she could take.

"No, I'm not too busy," she said, quickly scrawling Kevin's address on a piece of paper. She knew that wouldn't stop the girls from returning. She had the feeling that if they thought Lloyd was going to be around, they could become regular fixtures. "Here you go."

The pink-haired girl took the paper. Turning, she waved at Lloyd. "Bye."

"Good seeing you, girls." He smiled and waved back. Then he turned to Delaney. "Good seeing you, too." Before she could reply, he kissed her, a brief peck on the lips that left her wanting more. "I hope you don't mind my mowing the lawn. I had some free time and I figured I could use the exercise."

Exercise? He had to be joking. The man was already an Adonis. Now that he was standing closer she could see the sweat dampening his shirt. It added to his sensuality, as did the beads of perspiration streaming slowly down his face. He wore a wide handkerchief tied around his forehead, making him look incredibly sexy. No wonder the girls had been flirting with him shamelessly.

"You look hot," Delaney murmured. Would he kiss her again?

"I am. I've been working hard."

She cleared her throat and glanced away from him. "Would you like something cool to drink?" It was the least she could offer. "I could make some lemonade."

"Sounds great. I should finish up, though." He nodded toward the mower.

"Oh." She glanced at the lawn mower. "I can finish the lawn later."

"I'm almost done. It won't take me more than a few minutes. Why don't you make the lemonade?"

"Okay." A lame answer; she would be glad to get away. "Lloyd, how did you find my mower? I keep it locked in the garage."

"Actually this isn't yours," he said. "I borrowed this one from Mr. Peterson."

Mr. Peterson was the elderly man who lived across the street. Delaney glanced at the mower, seeing it for the first time. "Oh, I'll have to take some cookies over to him."

"For a mower?" Lloyd grinned. "Tell me, Delaney, what does the man who mows the lawn get?"

She smiled back at him. He was too sexy for his own good. "You can have some cookies, too."

"Gee, thanks."

Her smile broadened. "They're homemade."

"In that case I might take a look at your tail pipe, too. The girls were right. Your car sounds bad."

"Oh, was it the tail pipe that made all that racket?" she asked anxiously. She didn't know the first thing about cars. "Do you think it can be fixed?"

"I'll have to reserve my opinion until I take a look at it." He pulled the cord that started the lawn mower. Without a single hitch the thing roared to life. Whenever Delaney mowed the lawn, she pulled and pulled at the cord before the motor caught. He glanced at her and smiled again, and she realized she was staring openly and longingly at him. "Hurry up with that lemonade."

"Oh, right." Tearing her gaze from him, Delaney turned to go inside the house.

It took her longer than usual to make the lemonade. She got two phone calls, one from Jean and the other from someone trying to sell her aluminum siding. The home-improvement salesman was easy to dispense with. Jean, on the other hand, was persistent. When Delaney finally admitted that Lloyd was there, Jean hung up instantly.

By the time she went back outside, Lloyd had finished the mowing. He was lying on his back under her car, and Mr. Peterson was down on one knee beside him. The elderly man had lived across the street long before Delaney had moved in seven years ago. A widower, he was tall and wiry and white-haired, and for a man of seventy-six, he had no trouble getting around. He even dated an attractive widow on the next block occasionally.

Delaney set the cookies and lemonade on the porch and walked down the front steps to join the men. Mr. Peterson glanced up at her, shaking his head. "It's your crossover pipe this time," he said. "Lloyd's wiring it up for you so you can get to work tomorrow, but I think it's time you bought yourself a new car."

"You're probably right," Delaney answered as Lloyd extracted himself from underneath the Pinto, standing up in one lithe movement. She looked at him. "What do you think?"

"I agree with Fred," he said, wiping his hands on a rag. "The old gal may have character, but it's time to get rid of her."

Just like that? Delaney must have looked stricken, for Lloyd went on, "We can go see a dealer tomorrow night. I'll help you pick something out."

"Thanks." She knew as much about buying cars

as she did about fixing them. "What do you think I should get?"

"What else?" Mr. Peterson said. "A fancy sports car. Well," he went on, "now that we've got this figured out, I ought to get going. Emma's waiting for me. We're going to the carnival tonight."

"Emma?" Delaney was surprised. "I thought you were dating Mrs. Bostick."

"Nah, Sally and I broke up a couple of weeks ago. She's too wrapped up in her kids to be bothered with me."

Delaney smiled wryly at the older man's remark.

"Say, want to come along?" he asked abruptly. "We're going to have a good time."

"Sounds like fun," Lloyd said. "Maybe we'll meet you there. What do you think, Delaney?"

"You can't persuade Delaney to go." Mr. Peterson shook his head, a teasing glint in his eyes. "A carnival might be too much excitement for her."

"Mr. Peterson runs circles around me," Delaney explained.

Lloyd smiled. "I can believe it."

"But she's a good cook," Mr. Peterson went on. "Emma could use a few lessons in that department. She's too busy cavorting around all day long. Never did learn to fix a decent meal. Well, bye now."

"Thanks for letting me use your lawn mower," Lloyd called as Mr. Peterson hurried away. He glanced at Delaney. "Lemonade ready?"

She nodded. It was ridiculous, but now that it was just the two of them, she felt nervous all over again, wondering how to behave, what to say. When would he kiss her again? "Cookies, too."

"If you don't mind, I'll duck under the hose for a minute. Wash off some of this dirt."

"Fine." She thought he looked great just as he was, but she didn't say so. "I'll get you a towel."

When she got back a moment later, Lloyd was holding the nozzle of the hose over his head, letting the water run down over his chest and arms. Then he shut off the faucet and shook his head vigorously, sending droplets of water flying all around.

"Here." Delaney handed him the towel. Although he fluffed it through his dark hair, drops of water remained, glistening brightly in the sunshine. "Your shirt is wet," she pointed out.

He gave it a cursory glance. "I'll survive. In this heat it won't take long to dry. Ready?"

She was more than ready. She was willing and able, too.

Hold on, girl! Delaney stopped herself. She didn't want to get involved with Lloyd. Hadn't she told herself that over and over? So what if she was attracted to him? It had been so long since she'd had that kind of relationship, she wouldn't even know how to behave.

She turned to the porch, walking in front of him up the steps. Handing him a glass of lemonade and a cookie, she gestured toward an old-fashioned swing. "It's more comfortable than it looks."

He took a bite of cookie, then leaned down to steal another quick kiss before he sat in the swing.

"Delicious," he said.

She blushed. "Thank you."

Lloyd smiled and patted the seat. "Sit by me? I promise not to get you wet."

He didn't promise not to kiss her again. She sat

beside him, demurely tugging her dress down over her knees.

"I feel like I'm in another era," Lloyd said, placing his arm around her shoulder as he set the swing into slow motion with his foot.

"Why's that?"

"Here I am, a Marine, with a reputation to uphold. Two hundred years of pride and tradition and—"

"Womanizing?"

"Maybe." He grinned. "Anyhow, here I am having cookies and lemonade in a swing with a woman who blushes every time I look at her."

Delaney couldn't help blushing again. "The swing came with the house."

He tilted her chin so that she was looking at him. Close up she could see lighter flecks of blue in his eyes. They were so warm, so inviting. "And the blush?"

"It comes with the woman, I'm afraid."

"I'm glad. It's kind of nice, for a change." There was a long pause as he stared at her. He could weave magic with a single glance, she thought, wanting him to kiss her again. But Lloyd broke the mood. "I like to keep my promises, Delaney. If you come any closer you're going to get wet."

"Oh." She glanced at his shirt and pulled away.

"You could say it didn't matter."

She smiled. "But it does matter. I don't want to get wet."

He sighed and bit into his cookie. "Foiled again. These *are* good. Did you send any to Kevin?"

"I slipped a few into his duffel bag."

"They're almost worth going away for." Lloyd

paused again. "You know, you haven't asked about him today. Trying to let go?"

Trying, but not succeeding. Tears sprang suddenly into her eyes. Good Lord, this was ridiculous. Every time she was near this man she felt like crying. "Have you heard anything about him today?"

"I called Parris Island. All's well."

"Thanks."

"I won't call there again unless I have to. His drill instructor might give him a hard time if he thinks Kevin is getting some kind of special attention."

Delaney nodded. "I understand."

"Lemonade's good, too," Lloyd said after a moment. "It's fresh-squeezed, isn't it?"

"Yes."

"Sure tastes good."

There was another long pause and he took her chin in his hand again. "Don't be sad, Delaney," he said softly. "Come on, cheer up. Things are going to be fine."

"Are they?"

"Yes, they are," he said optimistically.

If only she could believe him. Somehow she was sure she would lose again—someone, something. Wasn't that what always happened?

"Hey!" he said, standing up abruptly and tugging her to her feet. "Enough sadness. Let's go to the carnival."

"I haven't been to a carnival in years," Delaney said uncertainly.

"Rides, cotton candy, and corn dogs. It'll be fun." He guided her toward the front door. "Mr. Peterson may be spry, but I'm a Marine. I'm not going to let that guy get the best of me."

Delaney surprised herself by laughing as Lloyd opened the door and tugged her inside.

"Grab a shower," he ordered, "and change your clothes while I put away the cookies and lemonade. We'll stop by my place so I can shower and change, too."

"I'll just be a few minutes." He was rushing her through the house so fast that she would have thought the carnival was some kind of military drill.

"We *could* save time and shower together." He paused and smiled suggestively. "I knew you'd blush," he said when her face turned pink. "It was just a suggestion, Delaney. We'll save it for another night."

Would there be another night? Delaney wasn't sure she could take that risk so soon. For the past few years her life had been so pleasant, so safe. Now all of a sudden she was being thrust into new territory, and she wasn't certain she could handle the anxiety.

"Better hurry," Lloyd said, "before I change my mind. Unless . . . could it be that you *do* want to shower with me?"

Abruptly, she turned away. "No vacancy," she told him. "You'll have to make reservations."

His low chuckle followed her from the room. "You know something, Delaney? You learn fast."

Chapter 4

LLOYD LIVED JUST a few blocks away from Delaney in a row of fashionable apartments. The landscaping of low, green shrubbery and leafy trees was meticulously maintained, and clumps of brightly blooming ornamental bushes flanked the entrance. They walked up the single flight of stairs, and Lloyd unlocked the door. Delaney was surprised at the elegant decor. Somehow Lloyd didn't strike her as the type of man who would take the time to pick out the thick beige carpet and well-upholstered chairs and sofas. The lamps appeared to be made of molded brass, and expensive-looking paintings adorned the walls. Delaney knew from experience that most military people led a more Spartan existence, collecting little

excess baggage—and certainly nothing costly—
since they moved so often.

"It's beautiful," she murmured, glancing around.
"How long have you been stationed in town?"

"Only a year." He tossed his keys on the polished
oak table. "But I can't take credit for the place. I'll
pass the compliment on to the landlord."

Delaney stared at him in disbelief. "This is a fur-
nished apartment?"

"Right down to the pots and pans."

She glanced around again, her suspicions con-
firmed. "So, even after nineteen years in the Marines
you can still pack all your belongings in a duffel bag
and be ready to get on a plane at a moment's notice."

"Yes," he answered, "I can. But believe me, Delaney, if I had a reason to put down roots, I'd do it,
whether or not I had to leave the next day."

She glanced at him again. This was the second
time he had admitted to being lonely. She wondered
if Lloyd regretted his divorce.

"Do you have a picture of your ex-wife?" she
asked abruptly.

"Amy?" He gave a short half-laugh, but his expression was almost bittersweet. "What brought that
up?"

"I don't know. . ." She wished she hadn't spoken
without thinking.

He shrugged. "I stopped carrying around pictures
of my ex-wife years ago."

"It's all right if you don't want to talk about her."
Delaney was curious, but deep down, she knew it
was more than curiosity that made her want to understand this man.

Lloyd shrugged as he lit several lamps. The room

took on a soft glow. "She was pretty. But it's been so long that I can't remember much about her anymore."

"How long have you been divorced?"

"Fifteen years, but that's misleading." He gestured toward the sofa. "Have a seat." When she was seated he went on, "Even though my marriage lasted for four years, Amy and I were only together for about three weeks."

"How come?"

"I was busy being a soldier."

"But she could have stayed with you," Delaney pointed out. "She could have lived on base."

"True." He shrugged. "Want something to drink? It's not fresh squeezed, but I do have some lemonade."

"That would be great, thanks."

Apparently his wife had chosen to live apart from him. Delaney had a feeling that had hurt him. She didn't want to ask, and in the end she didn't have to, for when Lloyd came back into the room and set the lemonade on an end table, he picked up the thread of the conversation easily. "And since my divorce there's been no one else. At least no one I've wanted to spend the rest of my life with. Amy made me realize I need someone very special. I've kept busy," he added, "by being stationed all over the world."

Delaney could understand that. She'd been alone all these years, and she'd kept busy, too. "On volunteer missions?"

"Yes."

"Richard always volunteered for everything."

"Kevin probably will, too, you know."

"Yes," she murmured, glancing down at the drink in her hand. "I know."

"I understand Kevin looks just like his father."

She glanced up, nodding. "Except that Richard was in the Navy. I can't imagine Kevin as a Marine." She frowned. "I wonder why he didn't choose the Navy?"

"Maybe he preferred the Marine Corps because it has two hundred years of pride and tradition."

She smiled. "Now you sound like a recruiter."

"Which I am." He smiled, too. "Actually, Delaney, Kevin and I discussed that. He wanted to be his own man. I know for a fact that he chose the Marines so he wouldn't have to follow in his father's footsteps."

"I suppose that was a wise decision."

"I think so," he agreed. "Are you planning to go to his graduation from boot camp?"

"I haven't planned much of anything," she admitted with a shrug.

"It's only been two days."

"So it's all right that I've been crying every night?" She smiled faintly.

"I'm saying it's to be expected. My mom cried, too, when I left for the Marines. I have a feeling all moms cry. But enough of this. Now"—he stood up quickly—"if we're ever going to get to the carnival I'd better take a shower. Make yourself at home; I'll be just a minute."

Delaney glanced at the magazines on the coffee table. Along with the usual men's assortment, there were a couple of military publications and two or three draft brochures. After leafing through *Sports*

Illustrated, she stood and went to the window to look outside.

A group of kids were playing baseball in the street. A female voice shouted for them to be careful —one of the mothers, probably. Delaney sighed, missing Kevin more than ever. She turned, her attention caught by a photograph. She picked it up and studied it. It was a picture of Lloyd with a young boy, both wearing camouflage fatigues. They were standing close together, Lloyd's arm slung over the boy's shoulder, and they were laughing.

Feeling as though she were intruding on something very private, she set the photograph back down and traced a finger over an elephant carved out of jade. The figure was far too expensive and fragile to be one of the rented furnishings. It was an odd piece; the clean, clear lines of the carving seemed to reflect Lloyd's personality.

As did the elegant curved swords hanging on the wall above, encased in glass. They had probably been used for ceremonies or parades, and had been carried by someone of very high rank. Delaney was certain the gold inlay was genuine on the swords. Tasseled loops of gold braid hung from the elegant hilt.

"In case you were wondering, those don't belong to the landlord," Lloyd said, entering the room. "They're mine."

Delaney turned to him. He wore dark, loose-fitting slacks and a light polo shirt. His hair was still damp from the shower. A single lock fell rakishly over his forehead.

"They're lovely," she answered.

"They were a gift from my commanding officer at Camp Lejeune."

He must have been quite close to the man. But she was surprised. "Camp Lejeune. Isn't that infantry?"

"Yes." Now he seemed surprised by her knowledge. "You've been holding out on me, Delaney. How do you know so much about Marine camps?"

"There were a couple of Marines in Richard's unit. A security detachment, I believe. He used to talk about them."

"Favorably, I hope?"

She smiled. "A Navy pilot?"

"I suppose not," he said. "Was he an Annapolis man?"

"Yes. Did you attend the Naval Academy, too?" Few people realized that academy graduates could enter either the Navy or the Marines after graduation.

"No, I worked my way up through the ranks."

"Isn't that hard to do in this day and age?"

"There are a few of us mustangs left."

"Then you must have trained at Parris Island."

He nodded. "Most recruits go through either Parris Island or the MCRD, San Diego."

She gestured at his clothes. "Going strictly civilian tonight?"

He smiled. "I thought you might be getting tired of all those emblems."

"Are you sure you don't have one or two tattooed on your chest?"

He laughed. "Don't worry, there's nothing on my chest except hair and nothing on my arm except my watch. Speaking of which"—he glanced down at his wrist—"if we don't get going, the carnival's going to be on its way to the next town."

With that he escorted her to the door. Delaney stepped in front of him on her way out, and he leaned down to brush his lips across hers. He kissed her again as he helped her out of his El Camino.

"Couldn't resist."

She just smiled. "I'll bet. Two hundred years of pride and tradition, right?"

He clasped her hand in his. "I think I'm going to regret that line."

The carnival was set up in the parking lot of the local high school, and it was packed. Delaney walked alongside Lloyd toward the midway, nodding to people she knew. Even in civilian clothes, Lloyd drew a number of appreciative stares. They had hardly arrived inside the gates when Lloyd bought four corn dogs, handing one to Delaney.

"It isn't burned, as you like, but it is a hot dog."

"This is better than a hot dog," she answered, sinking her teeth into the steamy crust. Perhaps it was the starry, clear night, or Lloyd's presence, but she felt strangely carefree. "Even burned. Mmmm."

"I gather I've discovered a weakness."

By mutual consent they had turned to continue walking. She looked at the three corn dogs in his hand. "Are you going to hoard those?"

"I suppose you're going to make me share?"

"Share or I'll take them away."

"You sound serious."

"Absolutely. You'll learn not to mess with a mother."

Lloyd laughed and handed over a second corn dog. "Who said women were the weaker sex? Any other food you especially like?"

"When it comes to cotton candy I'm no slouch either. How about you?"

"Love it," he said, "especially red."

"It appears we have something in common, Captain Thomas."

They were both done with their first corn dog. Lloyd smiled as he took her hand. "Come on, then, let's head for the roller coaster."

"Oh, no." Delaney pulled back.

"Don't tell me you don't like roller coasters?" He made it sound un-American.

"I've never actually been on one."

"How old are you?"

She shot him a dark look. "And just what does that have to do with it?"

"Nothing, really," he conceded. "You mean you never took Kevin on roller coasters when he was younger?"

"Absolutely not! I was a sensible mother."

"Well, you're not going to be sensible tonight," he said firmly. "Carnivals are supposed to be fun. So let's go."

Delaney didn't have much choice. Lloyd was already standing in line, and they were on the roller coaster before she could pull away.

He fastened her seat belt, and they started the long uphill trip, Delaney's heart already pounding with dread. Oh, Lord, what would the descent be like? Lloyd's laughter split the air, but when they reached the top and started down, Delaney screamed and clutched at his arm. "Lloyd!"

"Hang on, Delaney!"

For a minute she was too afraid to scream. Fortunately for Delaney, it was a modest roller coaster, and the ride was over quickly. Lloyd was still laughing when they got off. "Great, huh?"

"The best part," she gasped, "was getting off." She touched her chest where her heart was still beating frantically. "Oh, Lord, that was scary."

"Then we'll just have to go again," Lloyd declared, tugging her back into line. "Can't leave you with that impression. Roller coasters are fun!"

They went on the roller coaster four times. Delaney couldn't help it, she screamed at the beginning of each descent. Next they rode the Ferris wheel. Mr. Peterson and his friend passed them on the Tilt-a-Whirl. Lloyd insisted they stay on for another round, and they whipped by the other couple so fast that Delaney could only wave. They left at last when the carnival closed for the night.

They were walking to the car when someone called out to them. "Lloyd! Wait up, Lloyd."

They paused, and Delaney immediately recognized the young boy jogging toward them from the photograph in Lloyd's apartment. In the picture he hadn't looked quite so tall, and his hair hadn't seemed so blond and curly. The boy looked a bit sad, or perhaps he was just a serious kid, she thought.

"Curt!" Lloyd said, holding out his hand in greeting. "Good to see you. Sorry I missed you this morning." They clasped hands, and then Lloyd turned to Delaney. "Delaney Anderson, Curt Griffin."

"Kevin's mom, right?" Curt asked.

"Yes." Delaney nodded. That was one thing about living in a small town—everyone knew each other. She didn't remember seeing Curt before, but perhaps he hadn't been one of Kevin's closer friends. "It's nice to meet you."

"Yes, ma'am. You, too. Sorry to interrupt, but I wanted to check on the maneuvers this weekend." He turned to Lloyd. "Are we still on?"

"A group's going out. I'm not going to be able to make it, though," Lloyd answered. "I've got a couple of important meetings set up with some recruiters in downtown Chicago. Would you mind teaming up with someone else?"

"No problem. Maybe Jim will go. I'll see you when we get back on Monday, huh?"

"Sure thing. Hope it goes well." Lloyd patted the youth on the back like a proud father. "Stay alert!"

"Will do." He gave Delaney a half-salute. "Good to meet you, Mrs. Anderson."

Delaney smiled. As the boy waved and jogged away, she turned to Lloyd. "You seem very close."

He nodded, steering her toward his car. "We are. He lived with me for a while last winter," Lloyd went on, "until he patched things up with his stepsister."

"He lives with her?"

"Yes."

"Where are his parents?"

"Who knows?" Lloyd's tone was bitter. "The father was an alcoholic and the mother remarried, some idiot who doesn't like kids. They traveled a lot and Curt got in the way. Finally they tossed him out and he came here to live with his stepsister. She's all he has now but unfortunately they don't really get along. She's got her own family and doesn't have any time for him either."

"I thought there were laws to protect kids from things like that. Isn't it illegal to kick your own son out?"

"Yes, if the law's enforced. But Curt's probably

better off with his sister. At least he has some stability."

"And friends," Delaney added. "I guess you've sort of adopted him?"

Lloyd smiled. "Sort of. I suppose he's the son I never had. He's come a long way in just a few months."

"How did you meet?"

"I spend part of my leave each summer as a volunteer counselor at a camp for juvenile offenders," he explained. "And Curt had a long juvenile crime record."

Delaney wasn't surprised to hear that Lloyd devoted his spare time to helping troubled kids. "That must be very rewarding."

He shrugged. "It is. But I don't actually do much counseling. Mostly I build and run an obstacle course to help the kids work off their frustrations."

"Just being present and interested is a kind of counseling."

"True. It's sad that so many kids have no one."

"Like Curt?"

"We really hit it off," Lloyd said. "Even though he was a bit of a wise guy. Then we discovered we lived in the same town. It just seemed natural to do things together when we came home."

"What did he do that got him into a camp for juvenile offenders?"

"Petty theft, I think. The social workers tell me he was just going through a rebellion."

"And now?"

"Now he's clean. I think he's straightened out his life. At least, he's on his way. But it's too bad he doesn't have a real family."

"He has you."

Lloyd smiled. "Is that a compliment?"

"Yes."

"Thanks."

"I gather Curt's joining the Marines." Delaney surmised.

Lloyd shook his head. "Not just yet."

"Really?"

Lloyd smiled again. "He's signing right after summer school. He had to make up a credit he missed when he transferred here from Wisconsin."

"But you mentioned maneuvers."

"Every few weeks we take recruits out in the field to teach them some of the basics, especially if their entrance is going to be delayed or if they're undecided."

"Good recruiting tactics."

"Yes," Lloyd agreed. "And I'm not ashamed to admit it. We use a variety of tactics to attract recruits, especially in peacetime."

"I didn't mean to sound critical, Lloyd," Delaney said softly. "I was just thinking how sophisticated recruiting seems to have gotten. I know we need to have the military; we need a good defense system. But as the mother of a new recruit, I can't help resenting it."

"That's odd," he said thoughtfully, "I feel as though Curt is my son, but I'm proud of his decision to join the Marines." Lloyd paused for a moment as people milled around them. "Hell, maybe that's the recruiter in me talking," he finally said. "Maybe if Curt were really my son, I wouldn't feel that way."

"You do miss being a father, don't you?" Delaney wanted to touch him, to comfort him, tell him everything was all right. "You know it's not too late," she went on. "It's not as if you're an old man. You could still have a family."

"I suppose, if I found the right woman." He shrugged. "You really don't think I'm too old?"

"Not at all," she said. "What are you, thirty-seven?"

They had finally found the car; he helped her in and went around to his side as he spoke, "Thirty-eight." That meant he'd joined the Marines at nineteen. "Half my life is over."

"But you still have the other half."

"True," he said as he started the engine. "Tell me, we're around the same age. Would you want more children?"

"We are not the same age!" she exclaimed, darting him an angry glance. "I'm only thirty-four!" Almost thirty-five.

He laughed, a low, husky rumble in his chest. "I knew I could get you to admit your age sooner or later. Thirty-four, huh? Well, Delaney Anderson, you're fairly well preserved."

She knew he was teasing her. "Gee, thanks, Lloyd!"

His laugh rang out once more. "Sorry. I couldn't resist. You're always so serious. So what's the answer? Do you like babies?"

Delaney tried to answer honestly. "Sometimes I feel really ancient," she said, "and as the mother of an eighteen-year-old, I suppose I'd be a bit embarrassed pushing a baby carriage, but as Jean says—you remember Jean, the woman who works with me?"

"The tall brunette?"

Delaney nodded. "Jean says I'm a professional mother. I do love kids," she went on, unable to keep the wistfulness out of her voice. "So naturally I'd love a baby." *If I ever marry again. If I ever find someone to love.*

But she didn't say those words, and neither did Lloyd. For several long minutes she wondered if she should have kept silent. They didn't know each other very well and they had just broached a very personal subject. Not knowing what else to say, she folded her hands in her lap and looked out the window while he drove to her house.

"I'd love a baby, too, Delaney," he said softly, from out of nowhere.

She was even more uncomfortable. "Oh."

Thankfully he had pulled into her driveway. It was time to say goodnight; they wouldn't have to talk anymore. She wondered if he would kiss her. Since this afternoon when he'd come over to mow her lawn, he had just teased her with brief embraces.

"I'll pick you up after work tomorrow, okay? We'll go look for your new car."

He switched from one subject to the next so swiftly that Delaney didn't know what to think. "Fine."

"Have you decided what kind of car you want yet?"

"Something practical, I suppose," she said. "Maybe a small car would be best. They get good gas mileage."

"We'll look around."

Going to her side of the car, he opened the door and helped her out. They went slowly up the walk. Delaney's heart was pounding faster than when they'd first gotten on the roller coaster. What should she say? She felt shyer than ever. Why did the man intimidate her so?

"Well, good night," he said when they reached her door.

"Good night, Lloyd," she murmured. "See you tomorrow."

"You won't back out?"

She frowned, puzzled. "Why would I back out? I need a new car."

"I'm not talking about the car. I'm talking about us."

"Oh," she breathed. "Us?"

"Look at me, Delaney."

She did, and he kissed her, not one of the brief embraces he had been stealing all day, but a full-blown, sensuous kiss. Delaney felt her heart start to skip beats, and all she could do was cling to him as his lips plied hers, seeking, demanding, needing. As he crushed her along his length she could feel every inch of his lean, hard body.

At last he pulled away. "My," he said with a husky groan. "Good night again," he murmured. "Sleep tight."

She would probably lie awake forever and relive his kiss. "Good night, Lloyd."

"I have to leave."

"I know."

"Open the door and go inside."

"Okay." In a daze, she unlocked the door, opened it, and slipped inside.

It took Delaney a moment to realize that she was actually inside her house, safe and sound, and that Lloyd was outside, getting into his car and driving away. Taking a deep breath, she leaned against the door. She had to do something about Lloyd Thomas, and letting him kiss her wasn't the answer. He was more frightening than the roller coaster—and she couldn't, *wouldn't* get involved with him.

Tomorrow she would tell him she didn't need his help in buying a new car. She would stand on her own two feet. She was a capable adult and a mother, for goodness' sake! Only—she touched her lips wonderingly—she didn't feel like a mother when she was with Lloyd. When she was with Lloyd, she felt like a woman.

Delaney sighed and turned away from the door. Right now, she was a very confused woman indeed.

Chapter 5

DELANEY KNEW THAT vows were easy to make and hard to keep. Her decision to refuse Lloyd's help in buying a car was no exception. The next afternoon, he walked into the print shop, looking so tall and handsome that she forgot every objection she had planned to make. And Jean and Martin practically pushed her out the door.

"Go," Jean said when Delaney mentioned that it was only five o'clock. "If you don't buy a car soon, that rattletrap you drive is going to really break down. Then you won't be able to make it in, and I'll be stuck doing all the work around here."

"God help us all," Martin remarked.

Jean glared at him. "I don't need any comments

from the peanut gallery. Just print those flyers, buddy."

Delaney smiled at them. "You're sure you don't mind if I leave early?"

"Not at all."

"What about the bookmarks for—"

"Will you please go?" Jean waved her away.

They decided to leave Lloyd's car at the shop and take Delaney's, since she was going to trade it in anyway. As they walked across the parking lot together, Delaney pulled out her keys. "Do you want to drive?"

"You can have the final honor. By the way," he said, opening the door for her, "I didn't get a chance to say hello yet. How are you?"

She smiled as she swung inside the car. "Fine. And you?"

"Oh, I don't know, I've been kind of lonely." The car door was still open and all of a sudden he leaned down, his mouth just a few inches from hers. "I missed you today."

She had missed him, too. In fact, she had thought about nothing but Lloyd all day. And now he was going to kiss her. She stared up at him. "I—"

"Yes?"

She didn't get a chance to say more, for he brushed his lips lightly across hers, once, twice. The third time he lingered, deepening the kiss. Wisps of awareness raced along her spine and the world went spinning away as he brought his hand up to tenderly caress her cheek and then ran it down along her throat, to her arm, stroking her bare skin.

At last he drew back. She sighed. For a moment

she glanced out the window. "Oh, dear. Where were we going?"

He laughed. "The car dealer."

"Right." Obviously he thought she was teasing. She wasn't. She put the key in the ignition. "The car dealer."

Her Pinto was on its last legs, but it had been a good car, so Delaney decided to stop at a Ford dealership first. When they walked in, a tall, graying man spotted Lloyd and smiled, completely ignoring her. "May I help you, sir?"

"The lady is interested in a compact car."

The salesman turned his saccharine smile on her, and Delaney almost wished he'd stayed with Lloyd. "Need something practical, hm?"

"Practical" suddenly sounded like a bad word. But she nodded. "Yes. Something that will get good gas mileage."

"Well, we have plenty of cars, all with excellent mileage rates." The salesman led her to several small cars in the showroom, chatting all the while about their gasoline efficiency. His monologue grated on her nerves. Clearly this was a sales pitch he had used over and over again, and it sounded as tired as he looked. Lloyd was browsing through the rest of the showroom, and Delaney wondered if he'd had the foresight to anticipate what the man would be like, and if he had left her on her own on purpose.

She looked at one car after another. So did Lloyd, but he was scrutinizing sporty models. When the salesman had to answer a phone call she went over to where he stood beside a red Thunderbird.

"Nice," she murmured, glancing inside.

"Look at this, Delaney." He indicated the sleek,

state-of-the-art console. "When the gasoline is low, a drawing of a gas pump flashes on the screen. It also beeps."

"Convenient."

"Unless you happen to hate noise. You can turn it off, though." He stood back to take in the car as a whole. "Pretty color."

"Yes," she agreed.

"It suits you."

"Red? Me?" She stared at him. "I was thinking of brown."

"It's nice and small, too."

She glanced back at the car. "But it's a sports car."

"That it is. I happen to think Mr. Peterson was right. You definitely need something sporty. Come here," he went on, crooking his finger at her as he walked toward the back of the car. "Kick the tire."

"Why?"

"That's how you buy a car."

"I'm not buying a Thunderbird."

"Why not? They're not much more expensive than the cars you've been looking at."

She glanced at the price tag. Actually the bottom line wasn't too bad. She was already stunned by the prices she'd seen.

"But Thunderbirds aren't"—she had a hard time saying the word, after the salesman's speech—"practical."

"No, they aren't," Lloyd agreed. "Kick the tire."

Delaney stared at the car for a long moment. "Just kick, with my foot?" She felt foolish.

He nodded. "Just kick."

Two hours later Delaney Anderson drove home in her new red Thunderbird.

"It even gets good mileage," Lloyd said as she accelerated.

"It gets eighteen miles to the gallon, Lloyd."

"That's good mileage for a Thunderbird."

She laughed. "I suppose it all depends on how you look at it."

"Admit it, you love the car."

"Yes, I do," she said. She had rolled the windows down, and the wind was blowing through her hair. The radio was playing. She felt so daring. "I've never owned anything like it."

"I know." He smiled at her. "I bet there are a lot of things you've never owned . . . or done. So how about going dancing with me tonight?"

"Dancing?"

"I don't have to explain how you do that, do I, Delaney?"

"I know what dancing is, Lloyd. I was just surprised." She hadn't danced since the Boy Scout mother-son dinner dance four years ago, and she hadn't danced with a virile man since Richard was alive. She glanced at Lloyd. Even in the car he generated sex appeal.

"I thought we could celebrate the car," he went on.

"Where could we go?"

"Lots of places."

"But—"

"No buts, Delaney," he cut in. "We're going dancing right now."

Delaney was still wearing her work clothes: a pale blue shirtwaist dress and sensible low-heeled shoes.

And Lloyd wore his everyday uniform in olive drab and khaki. "Don't you think we should change clothes first?"

"No, I don't," he answered. "I think we should be impulsive. Let's go out to dinner first. There's a great little place close to here. Turn right at the next corner."

Delaney thought it over for a long moment. What harm could there be in having dinner with him and then dancing for a few hours? They were celebrating her purchase of the new car. Suddenly, being held in his arms was a most appealing prospect. She turned right.

The restaurant Lloyd chose was well known for its young, upwardly mobile crowd. Loud music throbbed from amplifiers on either side of a mirrored bar. Even the ceiling was mirrored over the dance floor. The atmosphere was dark, but strobe lights whirled around the room, throwing little diamond-shaped prisms across the floor. Since it was still early for dancing, there weren't many people waiting in line, and they were seated quickly.

"Do you come here a lot?" Delaney asked, glancing around.

"Not as much as I'd like to. I'm pretty busy at the recruiting station most of the time. Usually I grab a sandwich or something fast. I like to let the other guys get home so they can be with their families."

"That's nice of you."

He smiled gently. "Delaney, I told you, I'm a nice guy."

She was beginning to believe him. She smiled, too. "Maybe we'd better order."

While she was supposed to be studying the menu, Delaney studied Lloyd. So far he had worn both his dress uniforms, the blue and the white, and tonight he looked just as handsome in the olive drab and khaki working garb of a Marine.

They both decided on hamburgers for dinner, and Lloyd ordered wine with their meal. She lost track of the time as they ate and talked, Lloyd's car salesman imitation making her laugh out loud. Delaney held up her hand when he started to refill her glass for the third time. "If I drink much more I'll wind up under the table."

"After a dinner like that?"

They had consumed huge ground-beef patties with grilled mushrooms, onions, and melted cheese along with a platter of french fries. "I did make a pig of myself."

He laughed. "So did I. But don't worry about the wine. I'll drive. And we have to have Irish coffee to top off our meal. It's one of the house specialties."

"Sounds great," she said. "I love the whipped cream."

"Not to mention the Irish whiskey?"

"That's pretty good, too," she admitted.

The drinks came. They sipped their coffee for a moment. Then Lloyd set his drink down. "Come on, let's dance."

She glanced at the other people on the dance floor. "But this is a fast number."

She blushed instantly, realizing that she might as well have blurted out that she was looking forward to being close to him, to the feel of his body against hers.

"Can't you dance fast?" he teased, his eyes sparkling mischievously. He had obviously caught her blunder. "I thought you were only thirty-four."

"I guess age is irrelevant," she mumbled, even more embarrassed as he clasped her hand and led her onto the dance floor.

"Especially when your body's old and decrepit?"

"That's right."

"Speaking of which, I've just discovered I have this crick in my back," he murmured in her ear as they reached the dance floor. Taking her in his arms, he pulled her close. "It must be arthritis or old age setting in. I hope you don't mind. We'll have to dance slow."

She couldn't help laughing. So he wanted to be close to her, too. Several people stared at them, but she snuggled her head against his chest. It had to be the wine that was making her feel this way, or the Irish coffee. It wasn't like her to be so bold. "Only if you're sure it's because of your health."

"Oh, I'm positive," he said.

They danced slowly to that number and to every other number thereafter. Delaney wasn't sure how much time passed while they stayed on the dance floor, swaying softly to the music. She knew it was a very long time, but she was reluctant to move from Lloyd's arms. He felt so good, so lean and strong, that she could almost forget the things he represented, forget that he was a soldier, and that her son had gone away.

Kevin. For a moment she felt worse than a traitor. Her son had only been gone for three days, and she hadn't thought about him for hours now. She had also bought a new car, and now she was out celebrating with the enemy.

Lloyd must have sensed her mood change. He drew back. "What's the matter, Delaney?"

She shrugged. "People are staring at us."

"People have been staring at us all night. You're worried about Kevin, aren't you?"

How did he know? "I was just thinking about him. I still haven't heard from him."

"It's only been three days."

"I know." She couldn't tell Lloyd that she felt guilty; that would sound ridiculous.

But he must have guessed. He brushed a lock of hair away from her face and wiped the moisture from her eyes with his thumb. "You'll feel better if you go to the hardware store tomorrow and have a set of keys made for Kevin."

"To the new car?" She was amazed that Lloyd could read her mind.

He nodded. "Kevin will be coming home on leave eventually. Don't worry, Delaney. He'll love it when he finds out that you bought the car."

"Do you think so?"

"What kid wouldn't love a Thunderbird?" He held her close again. "Come on, let's dance some more."

"It's getting late, isn't it?" she said, but she snuggled against him.

"It's only two."

She drew back. "Two in the morning?"

He laughed. "It's certainly not the afternoon. What's the matter? Do you turn into a pumpkin at midnight?"

"No, but I'll sure feel like a pumpkin in the morning." She hadn't stayed up this late in years. Other couples were still dancing frenetically, looking as fresh as a bright summer day. She had gone to bed late last night, she told herself. Most of these people were young kids; they sure had more energy than she did. "Your car's still at the print shop," she said, just remembering Lloyd's vehicle. "We'd better pick it up."

"No problem. I'll pick it up tomorrow."

"How will you get home?"

"I can walk from your place. There's nothing wrong with my legs." There certainly wasn't. And there wasn't anything wrong with the rest of him, either. "Besides, I'm only thirty-eight," he went on as he led her from the dance floor. His eyes lit up playfully. "You're the old lady. I forgot you need your sleep."

"Who, me? Lloyd Thomas, I take back all the nice things I was thinking about you."

"What nice things?"

"I refuse to tell you. Besides, I always thought that when a lady went to bed it was called getting her beauty rest."

He leaned down abruptly and murmured, "In that case it's worked."

"Thank you."

"Forgiven?"

"Yes."

"You know, if you weren't so serious, I would have made a shocking remark."

"Which was?"

"I wouldn't mind getting some beauty rest with you."

"Lloyd!"

"Ah, Delaney," he laughed, "you blush so prettily. Hasn't anyone ever told you that you're desirable?"

"Not lately," she said seriously.

Suddenly he looked serious, too. "Well, you are. You're beautiful and you're very"—he swept his gaze over her body—"very desirable."

Things were moving too fast for Delaney. She wasn't ready for sexual advances. Lloyd must have sensed her discomfort, because he clasped her hand firmly in his. "But you're serious, so I didn't make that shocking remark. Come on, let's go. It's late and you're going to turn into a pumpkin."

Lloyd took her home. They chatted about the new car on the way, extolling all the different features. When they pulled into her driveway, Curt Griffin was sitting on the front steps.

"Something must be wrong," Lloyd said, frowning as they got out of the car. "Curt. Hello."

"I was hoping I'd find you here," Curt said. "I'm sorry to bother you again, Lloyd, and you, too, Mrs. Anderson." He nodded politely to her before turning back to Lloyd, his expression solemn. "But I was wondering if I could talk to you a minute."

"Have you been waiting a long time?" Lloyd asked.

Curt just shrugged. "I didn't mind waiting."

"You should have called Tom at the recruiting office. He could have told you where to find me."

"I didn't have anything else to do." Curt glanced at Delaney and gave her a small smile. "Besides, I figured you'd be with Mrs. Anderson."

Lloyd smiled, too, and nodded. "Okay," he said. "What's up?"

"I was wondering if I could bunk on your sofa again for a few days." Sighing heavily, the boy shoved his hands into his pockets. "My stepsister kicked me out again."

Lloyd's expression sobered. "What happened?"

"She got upset about something this morning. I don't really know what it was; she wouldn't tell me. Then I came in a little late tonight and the baby woke up. My sister starting yelling and just kicked me out."

"She'll probably calm down by morning," Lloyd said.

"I don't know," Curt answered. "She was pretty upset."

"Maybe the baby was sick or something," Lloyd suggested. "Or maybe it had just gotten to sleep when you came in."

"No, it's more than that this time."

"Did you do anything to make her angry?" Lloyd asked. "You know she doesn't like you to smart-mouth her."

Curt shook his head. "I didn't, honest." He sighed again. "I didn't want to bother you again, but it just hasn't been going well lately."

"What do you mean?" Lloyd asked.

"Well . . ." Curt shrugged. "Her husband's been complaining about me. He says they don't have any privacy. I just go there to sleep, and I try to stay out of their way as much as possible, but I guess I'm still an intrusion."

As the boy spoke, Delaney felt her motherly instincts take over. How could anyone be so callous? They had kicked the boy out because they wanted privacy? How could they have privacy with a baby around? Children always took up extra space. And if Curt was joining the Marines, he wasn't going to be around for very long, anyway. What was a few more weeks? Suddenly Delaney found herself disliking these people she hadn't even met.

"Have you had dinner?" she asked. "Do you want something to eat?"

"No, thank you, ma'am. It's late, and I've got maneuvers tomorrow." Curt glanced at Lloyd again. "I don't mean to be a pest, but do you think I could bunk with you, just for tonight?"

"You know you're always welcome at my place," Lloyd said. "Do you still have your key?"

"Yes, sir. I just didn't want to barge in without permission."

"You're not barging in, Curt. And you're not a pest. I'll meet you there, okay? I'll just take Mrs. Anderson inside."

"Oh, sure. Sorry." Curt blushed, apparently thinking he'd interrupted something. He clattered down the steps and went jogging into the darkness. "See you later."

Lloyd turned to Delaney, but he merely gave her a quick peck on the lips. Which was for the best, Delaney told herself as she got into bed a few minutes later, since she wasn't going to get involved with him. Sleep eluded her, though; all she could think about was why he hadn't really kissed her. He had told her she was beautiful and desirable, so why did he continue to act like a brother to her? Was he upset by her seriousness? That was something that would be hard to change. Or did it have something to do with Curt?

She was being ridiculous. She had known the man for only a short time. Did she want him to toss her over his shoulder and cart her into her bedroom? With a teenager in trouble standing there watching?

She sighed and turned over. The digital clock read 3:00 A.M. Deliberately she closed her eyes, but instead of counting sheep, all she could picture were tall Marines, all in the image of Lloyd Thomas.

An hour later the doorbell woke her. Delaney's immediate reaction was fear. All her life she had been conditioned to believe that doorbells and telephones ringing in the middle of the night meant disaster was calling. What had happened to Kevin? She had already forgotten him once tonight.

The bell kept on ringing. Finally she drew a robe around her and walked slowly to the door, feeling her heart break with each step. Let Kevin be all right. Please don't let it be someone with bad news. They always came in uniform, so formal, so rigid. They always murmured good day and asked polite little questions. And all the while you knew something was awfully, dreadfully wrong.

But when she finally pulled open the door, Mr. Peterson stood in the entrance. "Is that your car out there in the driveway?" he asked.

Delaney let her breath out all at once in a sigh of relief. "Yes," she said. "It's mine."

"Hot dog!"

Apparently that meant he liked it. "Mr. Peterson, what are you doing up this late?"

"I just got home."

"From a date?" she asked incredulously. "It's four in the morning."

. "Just because you come in when the chickens go to roost doesn't mean the rest of us do."

"True," she said.

"I was at Emma's. We were watching movies on the video recorder. Thought the darned things would never end." He paused and peered closely at her. "Did I scare you? You look upset."

"I thought something was wrong."

"So did I. I thought you had company, and I didn't think it was Lloyd."

So he had been checking up on her. "No, I don't have company."

"You never do, and it surprised the heck out of me when I saw that car. Thought I'd better come see. Well, you sure bought a nice-looking vehicle. I'll catch you tomorrow for a test drive. Okay?"

She nodded. "Great."

Delaney closed the door. This time she didn't have any trouble getting to sleep. But the phone rang less than an hour later, at five. For a moment she had that same instantaneous, fearful reaction. Then she snatched up the receiver.

It was Lloyd. "Delaney? I'm sorry to wake you," he said in his distinctively husky voice, "but I'm due downtown early and I knew I wouldn't get a chance to call you later. I just found your driver's license mixed in with some of my papers. The car salesman must have given it to me by mistake. I wanted to let you know in case you were worried."

Delaney sighed grimly. Once she had picked out the car, the salesman had wanted to deal strictly with Lloyd and it had seemed fruitless to object. "Oh, I hadn't noticed."

"I'll drop it by in the morning if that's okay."

What was wrong with tonight? Didn't he want to see her now? Or was he already doing something else? He *was* a bachelor. "That's fine. I'll try to catch a ride with Jean."

"I wouldn't go across the country, but you can still

drive," he said. "If you get stopped you just have to produce your license in court. I'd drop it over now, but I'm running behind schedule, and I won't get home until late tonight."

"Oh."

"You remember I have a couple of high-level meetings."

"Yes." He had mentioned them to Curt when he told the boy he couldn't go on maneuvers.

"Have a good day."

"I will, Lloyd, thanks. " When he hung up, she dropped the phone in its cradle and closed her eyes.

The alarm went off at six, and Delaney groaned. No matter what, she was going to bed early tonight! She would take Mr. Peterson for a test drive and then go straight to bed.

Martin and Jean were both eager to see her new car. They met her in the parking lot, oohing and aah-ing. "Hot number," Jean said, walking all around the automobile.

"Wow," was all Martin could say.

Delaney tossed him the keys. "Take it for a drive. It handles like a dream."

"Mmmh!" Jean exclaimed as Martin drove off. "Beautiful. Maybe I can get something like that when Adrienne finally flies the coup. Those experts all talk about the empty-nest syndrome, but I don't know. I'm sure looking forward to being alone. Sorry, Delaney," she said immediately. "I didn't mean to remind you about Kevin."

Delaney smiled. "It's getting easier."

"Well, he's all you've had all these years. I can understand why you'd miss him. But, boy, I sure won't miss the music and the friends and the damned telephone ringing all the time. And their rooms look like a pig sty." The two women stepped back inside the print shop. "Say, where did Captain Thomas stay last night? I see his car's still here in the lot."

Delaney glanced at Lloyd's El Camino. She wondered how he had gotten downtown; maybe he'd taken an official car. Her father always used to, and Lloyd was a captain. "He only lives a few blocks away from my house."

"Too bad," Jean sighed.

Delaney thought so, too; it was going to be a long day. "There's always another night."

Jean came to her desk and placed a hand on Delaney's forehead. "Delaney? Are you all right?"

She smiled. She had enjoyed shocking her friend. "Don't worry, Jean. I'm fine. Just tired."

Jean shook her head as she returned to her own desk. "Awfully tired, I'd say."

Delaney just laughed.

Chapter 6

THAT AFTERNOON A thunderstorm rolled in from the west. The print shop and most of the surrounding neighborhood lost electricity. Delaney had hated storms ever since she'd been in the middle of a hurricane as a child. She'd lived in southern Georgia with her parents then, near an Army base close to the Gulf of Mexico. Half the town had been destroyed. Delaney tried not to think about it; she spent the day cleaning out files, a chore that she and Jean had been putting off for months.

By the end of the day, Delaney wasn't nearly as tired as she had felt in the morning. After work, Mr. Peterson came over and they went for a drive in the new car. Later they sat on her front porch, watching the leaden clouds as they drank lemonade and ate the rest of the chocolate chip cookies.

"Heard from that boy of yours yet?"

Delaney shook her head. "It's only been four days." A lifetime to an anxious mother.

"Well, can't expect miracles, I suppose. What about Lloyd?"

"What about him?" Delaney was forced to ask when the old man didn't continue.

"Seems like a real nice guy. Noticed he pulled the weeds in your garden."

"Did he?" Delaney hadn't looked in the backyard in days.

"Yup. I went back there to get my lawn mower, and the weeds are all gone. Garden's even hoed."

"Didn't Lloyd return your lawn mower?"

"He wanted to change the spark plug for me."

"Oh." When had he done that? She tried to remember when Lloyd had borrowed Mr. Peterson's lawn mower. Maybe he had worked on it while she'd been changing her clothes so they could go to the carnival. "Did he change it?"

"'Course he did. Lloyd's a man of his word."

That was certainly true. Delaney took another sip of her lemonade. Thunder rumbled nearby; the deluge would probably start again soon. "Are you going out tonight?"

"Sure am. How about you?"

She shook her head. "I promised myself I'd stay in and get some sleep."

"Staying out too late these days, huh?"

"Yes."

Mr. Peterson took the last cookie from the plate.

"It's a good evening to sleep, rain and all, but I still say you need some more spice in your life."

He'd been telling her that for years; maybe it was time she took his advice. As Mr. Peterson stood up to leave she said, "Are you two watching movies again tonight?"

"No, Emma wants to go to a nightclub. There's a new band playing at Marengo's."

Marengo's was a local night spot; the place was always jumping. "Sounds like fun."

"Better'n bingo."

"I don't know about that," Delaney said. "I hear bingo's attracting a swinging crowd these days."

"Nah. That was me you've been hearing about. But I don't play any more. Too boring. Besides, Sally still goes to bingo. Can't take the new girl friend where the old girl friend goes."

Delaney laughed and waved as he headed across the street, covering his head with his hands to ward off the huge drops as the rain started up again. "Have a good time."

"You, too," he called back. "Say hello to Lloyd."

Delaney didn't know what to do with herself for the rest of the evening. She couldn't work in the garden; it was too wet. She wandered restlessly from one room to the next. Finally she made a fresh batch of cookies, wrapping up most of them to send to Kevin. She did set aside two plates, though, one for Mr. Peterson and the other for Lloyd.

She frowned when the doorbell rang a few minutes later. Maybe Mr. Peterson needed a ride somewhere. It had started to pour again. Wiping her sticky hands on a dish towel, she went to answer the door.

Lloyd stood in the doorway, still dressed in his fatigues, the shoulders of his shirt spotted with raindrops. A few raindrops clung to his dark hair. "Hi," he said in his honey-smooth, husky voice. "I got done early and thought I'd stop by. It's raining out."

That was an understatement. "Yes, it is."

"When the storm rolled in I knew I wanted to get done as early as possible. Sorry, this was the soonest I could come."

She was puzzled. "I wasn't going anywhere."

"I was hoping you weren't. I couldn't call."

"I thought you said I didn't really need my driver's license," she remarked.

They were still standing in the doorway. Lloyd smiled. "You don't. I came by so we could go for a walk in the rain."

"Oh," she said, even more surprised. "But I'm afraid of thunderstorms."

"Always?" he asked her. "This is such a nice storm."

What could possibly be nice about thunder and lightning and wind? "We'll get wet."

"That's the whole point."

"But it's so cold out."

"It's a little cool, but it feels good after that heat wave we had. Come on, Delaney," he went on softly. "Live dangerously for once."

What did he want from her? She'd already bought a sports car. She'd gone dancing. She'd taken up with a Marine—and she'd loved every moment of it. But she hated thunderstorms. "Hang on. I'll get a raincoat."

He held out his hand when she came back. "Let's try to run through the drops."

The man had some strange ideas, Delaney thought as they clattered down the front steps and onto the sidewalk. The rain was coming down steadily, and it was completely dark outside, with only the streetlights illuminating the area. A heavy mist rose from the ground like a veil.

"We'd better hurry," he said, tugging her along beside him as he broke into a slow trot, "so most of the drops will miss us."

That would be quite a trick. Occasionally a car splashed by them, but few people were out in the downpour. Delaney couldn't get her raincoat snapped and within moments they both were drenched. Yet it was almost pleasant outside, Delaney thought as she ran alongside of Lloyd. The wind was behind them; the thunder was far off in the distance. The night was soft and the raindrops felt silky on her face.

They headed down the suburban street, pushing low-hanging tree branches out of the way as they ran. Water splashed off the boughs in huge drops.

"Oh!" Delaney cried when Lloyd pushed aside a large branch, dumping most of the water down the back of her neck.

"Did you get wet?"

She laughed. "Soaked."

"Hurry," he said again, increasing his speed. "Run faster."

Delaney ran, her hair streaming out behind her, her clothes completely drenched, and her breath coming in gasps. Yet she felt strangely exhilarated—alive.

There was a park a few blocks from her house. Still running, they crossed a busy street and headed down the soft, bark-strewn path. The trees grew denser here, and several willows, limbs bowed to the ground, circled a small lake.

"Tired?" Lloyd asked.

By now Delaney was almost completely out of breath. "Yes."

"Want to stop?"

"Not yet."

They headed down the soft bark-strewn path that led deep into the park. They tramped through a puddle, splashing water up, and Delaney cried out again. At that precise moment the heavens opened with a deluge, and the rain drove down in sheets. Delaney laughed in spite of herself. "Lloyd!" she squealed. "I'm so wet!"

"Come on," he said, pulling her beneath the branches of a tall willow tree, "let's dry off for a bit."

The thunder and lightning had stopped, so Delaney knew they'd be safe under the large willow. She shook water from her hair as she leaned against its trunk.

"Having fun?" Lloyd asked.

She glanced up at him and smiled. Rain dripped from his hair, too, and streamed down his cheeks. "Yes. Thank you for asking me to walk in the rain."

"You're welcome."

"We should get back, though."

"We can catch a cab."

She peered out of the branches at the deserted street. "Where?"

"We'll find one."

She glanced back at him. "You're always optimistic, aren't you?"

He shrugged. "Why not? Things generally work

out." He pushed a wet lock of hair away from her face. Water dripped down on her neck and back in a steady stream. "Cold?"

"No." The branches enveloped them in a warm cocoon. And Lloyd was close to her; she could feel the heat from his body.

"Are you sure? Your lips look cold. They're turning blue."

She was leaning against the tree and he stood in front of her, hands spread on the trunk behind her shoulders. *You could warm them up.*

"Maybe a little," she said.

Lloyd must have read her mind, for he leaned down, brushing his lips gently across hers. His breath was moist against her mouth, his lips wet, yet soft and warm.

"You are cold," he murmured huskily as a shiver snaked through her. "We'd better get back. I don't want you to catch a cold."

Don't stop! she wanted to cry out. *Kiss me!* But she drew a deep breath and followed as he took her hand to lead her from the park.

Amazingly, when they got to the street, a cab was passing. Lloyd gave a loud whistle and the driver braked to a halt.

"I think you set this up," Delaney said as they ran for the vehicle. "There are never any cabs around here."

"I live right," he answered, ushering her quickly inside and diving in behind her. "Turn on the heat," he said to the cabbie after reciting her address. "We're wet."

"You ain't just wet," the man said, "you're

soaked. How'd you get caught in this downpour? They been forecasting a storm all day long."

"We went for a walk."

"In the rain? What are you, crazy?"

"It was his idea," Delaney said, smiling at Lloyd.

He laughed and flicked water at her. "Actually the lady forced me out in the cold and rain. She wanted to try to run between the raindrops."

The cabbie just shook his head in disbelief.

Delaney scowled at Lloyd playfully and flicked some water back at him. By the time they pulled up in front of her house, they were both shivering. She waited while he paid the driver; then they got out quickly and ran up the steps to her porch. Delaney unlocked the front door and they rushed inside.

"Go jump in a warm shower," Lloyd instructed. "And bundle up. I'll get a fire going."

One of the nicer features of the old house was the huge stone fireplace in her living room. "A fire sounds like a great idea." She nodded approvingly, her teeth chattering. "It's so cold that I can't believe this is July!"

"Feels like March. Where's your firewood?"

"Around the side of the house."

She felt sorry for Lloyd as he headed back out into the rain—but not sorry enough to help. She set a few towels near the door and darted into the bathroom.

The hot water felt wonderful streaming over her, and she sighed with delight, wanting to stay under it forever. Afterward, she didn't feel like really getting dressed. All she wanted to do was curl up in front of the fire Lloyd was building. She wriggled into her heavy chenille robe, wrapped a towel around her hair, and went into the living room.

Lloyd had lit a few lamps, and a fire was already crackling in the fireplace, throwing pale orange light into the room. Lloyd had rubbed his hair with a towel and had taken off his shoes and his shirt, but his T-shirt was still soaked, and his pants dripped water.

"I think you've ruined your uniform."

He glanced down. "The local dry cleaner works miracles. I'll take it in in the morning."

"Would you like to take a shower, too?"

"I'll be fine," Lloyd said. "If you've got another towel, I'll just wipe off my pants so I don't drip all over the rug."

"Oh, sure."

"Got a blanket as well? I'll spread it on the floor in front of the fireplace, and we can dry off by the fire."

Delaney brought him both. "I could make some hot chocolate."

"We should probably start drinking orange juice and taking aspirin," he said, "to ward off the terrible colds we'll be getting. But hot chocolate sounds great."

"Do you think cognac would taste good in it?" she asked, pausing. "I have some in the cabinet."

"Cognac?"

"I don't have to explain what that is, do I?" she asked, teasing him.

"No, you don't have to explain it. You just don't strike me as the type to drink cognac."

"I'm not. I use it for baked Alaska."

He smiled. "In any case I think it would taste great in hot chocolate."

While Lloyd spread the blanket and tended the fire, Delaney made their drinks. She brought a plate of cookies, too. Lloyd was stretched out in front of the fire. She started to sit on the sofa just behind him when he patted the blanket. "It's warmer down here."

It looked cozier, and without a moment's hesitation she sat beside him, handing him his mug of hot chocolate. "By the way, how's Curt?"

Lloyd shook his head as he took a sip. "He called his stepsister this morning, but she wouldn't talk to him. I think he's going to be staying with me this summer."

"You don't sound like you'll mind that too much."

"He's a great kid," Lloyd said. "I can't understand why he has trouble getting along with his family."

"Maybe it's not his fault."

"Maybe not," Lloyd agreed. "Have you heard from Kevin yet?"

"No," she said softly.

"The mail's slow sometimes."

"Maybe." She twirled the mug around in her hands, staring into the dark liquid. "Maybe he hasn't written."

"I'm sure he has by now," Lloyd said, leaning back and propping his head on his elbow. "Kevin knows you're waiting to hear from him, but he's probably too tired to do much writing."

She glanced at him. "When you were a recruit, did you write home a lot?"

"I wasn't much of a letter writer. I guess my mother waited by the mailbox, too."

He had probably been a hell raiser, Delaney thought, out wooing the girls in town whenever he could get away. "How about now?"

He shook his head. "I usually phone."

"So do I. Do you see your folks often?"

"I go home about once a year on leave," he said. "I'd like to visit there more often, but I can't."

"Where is home?" she asked curiously. "Didn't you say you were from North Carolina?"

He nodded. "A small town on the coast, near Cape Fear—our only claim to fame."

"Cape Fear? That sounds like a pleasant place!"

"Actually, it's pretty treacherous. It's a promontory on the southern tip of Smith Island that juts into the Atlantic. When I was a kid I used to row my boat out there just to tempt fate. I'd get caught in the current and then fight like crazy to get back to shore. Once I went out in a storm and almost didn't make it back at all."

"I guess you really like storms."

"Not always." He smiled. "I guess I just like pitting myself against the elements."

Delaney nodded. She had felt some of that kind of exhilaration tonight, in the rain. "When I was caught in that hurricane, it gave me great respect for the unpredictability of nature."

"I can imagine," he said. "I've been through a couple of hurricanes myself. And a lot of ordinary storms, too. I remember always being wet when I was a kid—I felt like a frog."

"Who turned into a prince?"

He laughed. "Think so?"

"You're very handsome," she said honestly. In fact, at the moment he looked devastatingly attractive. In the firelight his dark hair appeared burnished, almost coppery. His T-shirt had dried and stretched tautly across his broad chest. The white cotton contrasted with his tanned skin.

"Just like in the fairy tale?"

If only life were really like a fairy tale. "Yes, just like that," Delaney said.

"As I remember the fairy tale, the frog didn't turn into a prince until he was kissed by a beautiful princess."

Delaney blushed and looked down at her mug of hot chocolate.

"But I always wondered if she kissed him again if he'd turn back into a frog," Lloyd continued.

She laughed. "I don't know. Are you afraid you'll turn back into the little boy you were on Cape Fear?"

"I think I'm on my way." He set his empty mug down on a table. "That was good."

"Warm, at least," she said.

He nodded. "It's starting to feel very warm in here." The towel had fallen off her head and he reached out to touch a lock of hair that lay over her cheek. "Your hair's dry. It's curly."

She had felt so at ease with Lloyd that she had forgotten to worry about her appearance. "When my hair gets wet it always gets like this."

"It's beautiful," he said huskily, sifting his fingers through the long strands and letting them fall onto her shoulders. "So long and silky."

Delaney didn't know what to say. "I— Thank you."

"You still have trouble accepting compliments, I see."

"I guess old habits are hard to break."

"But trying to break them can be interesting," he murmured, still running his fingers through her hair.

"I suppose," she said softly.

Taking her mug from her hand, Lloyd set it beside

his and leaned toward her. Everything in the room was bathed in a soft orange glow. Behind them, the fire crackled, but Delaney saw only Lloyd as he came closer.

"Let's try," he whispered. "Then we'll know for sure."

He was going to kiss her. Slowly, so slowly that she could count the endless seconds, his lips descended on hers. Soft at first, his mouth grew hard and demanding against hers. As he pressed closer, a fiery glow flickered through her limbs, feather light but wild as a tempest. With a tiny gasp of surrender she entwined her hands in his hair and pressed close to him.

Lloyd groaned and deepened the kiss, running his hands along her back, through her hair. All she could think of was the feel of his lips, soft and warm; the strength of his arms; the firm length of his body pressed against hers; the heat of his flesh scorching her skin. A white-hot blaze burned inside her, raging out of control.

"Delaney," he murmured thickly.

Time seemed to stop as he moved his lips commandingly over hers. The moments blended into forever as Lloyd entwined his hands in her hair and kissed her eyelids, the slope of her neck, tracing a path of caresses down the front of her robe to the slight rise of her breasts.

"Oh, God, Delaney."

"Lloyd," she whispered back.

Her robe fell open and he cupped her breasts with his hands. She arched against him, seeking, needing. Soon his lips replaced his hands and she gasped with sweet agony as he took first one nipple and then the other in his mouth, suckling gently. He trailed a tempestuous path across her body, his breath hot and harsh against her skin. When his fingers stroked her stomach and touched the mound of silky hairs, she cried out softly with a combination of shock and delight. It had been so long since she'd felt a man's touch, so very long.

"Delaney? Do you want me to stop?"

His voice came to her as though in a dream, and all of a sudden she shuddered with fear. Fear of letting herself go, of loving, of caring again—of Lloyd. It pounded through her in a frantic rush.

Oh, Lord, what was she going to do? She couldn't let him penetrate her defenses. She was still too vulnerable. There was a pattern to her life that she didn't want to keep on repeating. She couldn't bear to lose again, to lose someone she might love.

Lloyd paused, as though sensing her withdrawal. "What's the matter, Delaney?"

"I—I don't know," she murmured. She had led him on, had let him kiss her, caress her. What kind of woman was she? "I'm sorry, Lloyd."

"Are you frightened?"

"Yes." *Oh, Lord, yes.* She was petrified—of Lloyd, of being hurt.

"I won't hurt you."

Maybe not on purpose. But she couldn't take the chance. She couldn't let this happen. She sat up, pulling her robe closed. "I'm sorry. I can't—" But she couldn't finish.

He sat up beside her, stroking her hair gently. "Is it me?"

"No!" How could he even think that?

"Then what's wrong, Delaney?"

She buried her head in her hands. "I don't know. I guess I'm just not ready."

He studied her for a long moment. She could feel his gaze, his eyes assessing her. Then, with a sigh, he reached for her chin and tilted it in that special way of his, so that she was looking up at him. He kissed her chastely on the mouth. "I'll see you tomorrow. Okay?"

She felt even worse. "Lloyd—"

"Don't worry, Delaney, I understand. When we make love . . . and I will make love with you," he went on softly, like a promise, "it will be special for both of us."

Why did he have to be so nice? She stood up and pulled her robe tightly around her waist. She wanted to throw herself into his arms. She wanted to tear off her robe and press against him, to let him touch her, kiss her, make love to her.

"I've led you on, Lloyd. I—" She had practically thrown herself at him; she felt so ashamed. "I—I let you . . . touch me."

"I've led *you* on," he countered.

She smiled at him, at his gentleness. How could he be so strong and yet so gentle? She was a thirty-four-year-old woman; she had a grown child. She had suffered other hurts before. Why was she so afraid?

Because she had learned that just when you were ready to trust again, a hurricane could come along. After a while you learned to stay away from thunderstorms.

"I feel so stupid."

He folded her in his arms, comforting her. "You aren't stupid, Delaney. I respect you, and I don't mind waiting." Very softly he added, "And when you're ready, I'll be here."

Chapter 7

SATURDAY DAWNED BRIGHT and sunny. Delaney only had to work a halfday at the print shop; the boss liked to close early on the weekends. She stopped at a grocery store on the way home, and when she walked up her front steps, she found a letter from Kevin in her mailbox. She dropped the bags of groceries and ripped the letter open right there. Mr. Peterson saw her from across the street and guessed the news. He hurried to her side and started reading over her shoulder.

"Sounds like he's doing fine," the old man said after a moment.

"He says the food is good."

"Kevin always did eat everything, anyhow."

That was true; even as a child her son had been easy to please. "He says next weekend he's going to have a few hours' leave off base," Delaney said. "A bunch of guys are going into town."

"Now you've really got something to worry about."

Delaney smiled. "Do you think he'll meet a nice girl?"

"I hope so," the old man said. "Just hope he uses his head about it."

Delaney hoped so, too. She wished she could learn to do the same, instead of letting her emotions sweep her away on a tidal wave, like last night. She had come very close to letting Lloyd make love to her, letting him become part of her life. And she certainly couldn't do that. Not now.

When he rang her doorbell a few hours later, Delaney couldn't help being glad to see him. "Hi, Lloyd." She smiled, holding out Kevin's letter. "It came."

"A letter from Kevin?" he asked, his face lighting up with a grin. "So soon?"

"Soon? It's been five days!"

Lloyd laughed. "A lifetime."

"You're not a mother."

"I'm glad."

She wrinkled her nose at him and pulled the already frayed pages out of the envelope, handing them to him. "He says the blankets on his bed have to be so tight that his drill sergeant can bounce a quarter off of them."

"I'm surprised you didn't know that rule," Lloyd said, taking the letter from her. "Weren't you raised on Army bases?"

"Yes, but I had forgotten a lot of the spit and polish."

"He gets leave next weekend, huh?"

"Mr. Peterson says that means trouble."

"Probably," Lloyd agreed. "But it won't do you any good to worry about it. You can't do a thing."

"I suppose that's true." She laughed again. So what if Kevin went into town? He was a smart boy. "He sounds good, Lloyd."

"He'll be fine."

She glanced at Lloyd. Maybe she would be fine, too. She still felt uncomfortable thinking about the previous evening. He had left soon after she rejected his advances, and they hadn't really talked. She still had no idea what to say. How did you broach the subject? *Oh, by the way, about last night, sorry I acted like such a prude but if you touch me tonight I'll probably do the same thing again?* Or, *You'll forgive me, it's been a long, dry spell and I don't know how to act around men.*

Lloyd spoke first. "Doing anything tonight?"

Delaney knew she should have said yes. She should have told him to go home, to stay out of her life. Instead, she shook her head. "Nothing special."

"There's going to be a full moon."

She smiled. "We've already established that I turn into a pumpkin late at night. Do you turn into a werewolf when the moon is full?"

"Fangs and all." He pretended to growl. "I thought we might go swimming."

He certainly liked water. "Tonight? Where?"

"My apartment complex has a pool. What do you say?"

"Let's wait until it's dark, so we can swim in the

moonlight," she said. "In the meantime we can bake cookies or brownies or something."

"Brownies sound good. I'll help." He began rolling up his sleeves.

The man didn't give up. Didn't he mind the fact that she had led him on and then developed cold feet?

"What about last night?" she asked abruptly.

He didn't even pretend he didn't know what she was talking about. He glanced at her but kept rolling up his sleeves. "I told you I was willing to wait until you were ready—whenever that happens."

"That's the problem, Lloyd," she said softly. "I don't know if I'll ever be ready to—"

"You need time, Delaney. That's all."

She wished it were that simple. And Lloyd didn't strike her as a particularly patient man. He was someone who challenged the unknown, who took risks. "Are you saying you're ready to settle in for a long wait?"

He smiled again, that slow, easy grin that softened the lines of his face. "You remember the storm I told you about last night?"

"The one when you were a kid? On Cape Fear?"

He nodded. "I knew it was coming and I waited for it. I rowed out there in the currents and I waited and waited until it finally hit. You're like that storm, Delaney."

"A challenge?" She wasn't certain she liked the comparison.

"Maybe a challenge at first," he said, "but much more than that in the end, something to remember forever. There's something about you that's still . . . unawakened, Delaney," he went on, sensing her puzzlement. "Something gathering, something elemental and very, very wonderful, and one moment, just like that storm, it's going to hit."

She looked at him in surprise. "Are you sure you can handle that challenge?"

To her surprise he laughed. "Oh, hell, I don't know. What do you say we forget all this nonsense and bake some brownies?"

But she couldn't let it go so easily. She glanced down at her hands. "I don't know what's the matter with me."

"Fear," he said.

"Of getting involved?"

"Of loss. You have to take risks before you can lose, Delaney, but you have to take them to win, too."

"I know," she said softly.

"Are we going to bake some brownies?"

"Sure." She got out a pan and turned on the oven. Wanting to change the subject, she asked, "Where's Curt?"

"At my apartment."

"Has he eaten?" She glanced at Lloyd. "I could cook dinner, if you're hungry."

"Would you mind?"

"Lloyd, you know I'd be delighted." She smiled. "Call Curt and tell him to come right over."

Delaney barbecued steaks. They ate the brownies for dessert; Lloyd's batch had burned slightly, and Curt teased him. Once again Delaney noticed how close the two of them had become. Curt didn't seem nearly as serious as he had that first night she'd met him. Maybe his argument with his stepsister had made him appear reticent, for tonight he seemed witty and outgoing. And frank, she discovered when Lloyd went inside the house for a refill of coffee.

Curt turned to Delaney. "Captain Thomas told you I was in jail, didn't he?"

Delaney studied him for a long moment, not knowing how to answer him. "Lloyd mentioned that you met at a camp for juvenile offenders."

"I was in jail before that. If I hadn't met Lloyd I'd probably be doing hard time in prison by now."

"You were really in a lot of trouble?" Lloyd had made it sound as though the boy had only been in minor skirmishes with the law.

"I stole some things, but I would have gotten into worse trouble sooner or later. I was headed that way. You know," he went on, "it's easy for a kid to get messed up."

He meant without parental guidance, Delaney knew, and she couldn't have agreed with him more. She had always been thankful that Kevin hadn't tested the limits, especially without a father. He had always been such a good son.

"Yes, it is easy to get messed up," she said. "But the important thing is that you've got your life back on track."

"I understand you don't like the Marines."

She hesitated a moment. "It's not just the Marines. It's the military in general."

"Lloyd told me you lost a lot of people you cared about."

"Yes, that's true."

"I'm going to college, Mrs. Anderson. I'm going to be somebody, and it's because of the Marines that I'm going to be able to do it."

"I understand that, Curt," she answered softly.

"But you see, my hurt has nothing to do with what the military can give a person. My hurt comes from what the military has taken away."

He seemed to ponder her words. Finally he nodded. "I hope I didn't upset you. Maybe I shouldn't have said anything. My sister always says I've got a big mouth. It's just that I really admire Lloyd, and I needed to know how you felt."

"I understand that, too."

He laughed. "We both understand a lot, huh?"

She smiled. "Yes, we do."

"You don't mind that Lloyd and I talked about you?"

"No. I'm glad you two are so close." She refilled his glass with lemonade. "So what are you going to study in college?"

"Engineering. If I can do it." He grinned. "Lloyd says I can do anything I set out to do."

"He does believe that," Delaney agreed, remembering that first night they'd met when he had talked about people's aspirations. "So do I," she added abruptly. Perhaps it was Kevin's letter that was beginning to make her see the truth in Lloyd's outlook. Her son was growing up, and suddenly she did believe he could do anything he set out to do. Maybe she could, too.

Lloyd came back outside then and they launched into a rousing game of croquet. Lloyd beat both Curt and Delaney soundly.

When Curt had left, Lloyd turned to her. "Ready for that swim?"

It was late, but she didn't care. "I think you have a fetish for water."

"I told you I was once a frog."

She laughed. "I'm starting to believe it."

"Come on, the moon is full."

And the night was magic, so soft and sensual.

The pool at Lloyd's apartment complex was large and totally private, surrounded by foliage. Tonight it was completely deserted.

While she waited, Lloyd went upstairs to change into his swimming trunks. When he came back, Delaney could see what a magnificent body the man possessed. This was the first time she had seen him without a shirt. Thick, dark hair curled across his chest and arrowed down beneath his waistband. She had a sudden urge to touch him, to run her fingers across that chest and down that thin line. Readjusting her suit, she flushed at her own thoughts. Next thing she knew she would be attacking him.

Lloyd leaned down and whispered, "I like your suit. It shows off your legs."

Did he know she had been looking at him, too? "Thanks. You don't look so bad yourself, for an old man," she couldn't help adding.

"Touché." Smiling, he took her hand. "Ready for the water? Grit your teeth."

They jumped in together. The water was *cold*. Quickly Delaney stroked to the other side of the pool. She surfaced, sputtering and shivering. "Oh! It's freezing!"

Lloyd had swum alongside her. He pulled her into his arms and started to rub her shoulders with his hands. "I guess I'll just have to keep you warm. It's the gentlemanly thing to do."

Despite the cold, Delaney laughed. Since when were Marines so gallant? "Oh, really?"

"And you do know that the best way to keep

warm is body heat," he went on, tucking her close to him. She could feel every inch of his body, the muscled hardness, the smooth expanse of cloth. "You don't mind, do you?"

They were so close that the slightly rough hair on his legs prickled her. "Of course not," she said, "but I thought you were going to be patient with me."

He nodded. "I am being patient. I said I'd wait until you were ready to be closer. I *didn't* say I'd do it chastely."

She laughed. "Is there a difference?"

"There is. Delaney, put your arms around me. I'm going to kiss you."

She did.

And, oh, what a kiss. It tingled her lips and sizzled her blood as he pulled her tightly against him. When he slipped his hands over her breasts, she was suddenly very warm. They sank under the water, lips and limbs still entwined, kissing until she thought she might drown.

"Well?" he said when they broke the surface and gasped for breath. "Still cold?"

"No," she murmured, smiling devilishly, "but I feel a shiver coming on."

He laughed. "Oh, Delaney, I think I love you." And he kissed her again.

It was just a word, an endearment, Delaney told herself. And at the end of the night, at her front door, he was the perfect gentleman. He didn't even ask to come in. "One day you'll ask me," he murmured, nuzzling her lips. Then he was gone.

Delaney leaned against the door and sighed. She was either the luckiest woman in the world or the unluckiest; she didn't know which. And right now she was too cónfused to try to figure it out.

The next day they went canoeing down the Des Plaines River. She teased Lloyd again about his fetish for water; on Monday after work, they went horseback riding for a change of pace. On Tuesday they played miniature golf; on Wednesday Lloyd took her to the zoo. They wandered among the animals, laughing and making faces, eating cotton candy and hot dogs. On Thursday they took Curt to the movies. Delaney felt protective of the teenager, not just because Kevin was gone but because the boy had a certain wistful charm of his own.

But it was strange having Lloyd around the house all the time. Delaney had been alone for so long. Now she felt as though they were a couple; she was becoming more and more aware of him as a virile man. Now she waited for him to touch her, kiss her, and each time she saw him she lost more of her heart to him. A storm was gathering, and she didn't know how to stop it. She wasn't sure she wanted to stop it. Lloyd Thomas was the most fascinating man she had ever met. He was also the most energetic. By the end of the week Delaney swore they had done every single thing there was to do in the world. He had to agree.

"The only thing left is lovers' lane," he teased when he came by on Saturday night. "Any ideas?"

"Lovers' lane sounds like fun," Delaney said boldly.

He looked at her. "Delaney, I don't think I could take going to lovers' lane with you."

"Thanks a lot. And what's the matter with me?"

"Nothing's the matter with you," he said. "You're

beautiful. I'm just not sure I'm up to a make-out session."

She smiled. "We can always walk around the lake."

"And look at the beaver dams?"

"Doesn't that sound like fun?"

He laughed. "That's really where you want to go?"

"Can we?" she said excitedly.

It must have been the animated sparkle in her eyes that convinced him. Shaking his head in bewilderment, Lloyd finally said, "Sure. We'll go."

Lovers' lane was crowded. They had taken her Thunderbird, and Lloyd pulled into a spot between two other cars. The only way Delaney could tell there were bodies inside the other cars was by the slight sway when the occupants shifted position.

"Well, here we are," Lloyd said grimly, shutting off the engine.

"Is it that bad?"

"Delaney, being here with you is going to be torture," he said. "I don't think I can keep my hands off of you."

"Then don't," she said softly.

For a moment he didn't say anything. Then he murmured, "Pardon me?"

She drew his hand to her lips and kissed his palm. "Then don't."

Lloyd hesitated. "What are we going to do about the stick shift?"

Delaney glanced down. Why had she bought a sports car? It made things so complicated. "Climb over it?"

"You're serious about this, aren't you?"

"Making out?" Delaney smiled at him sweetly.

"Yes."

"Dead serious."

Drawing a deep breath, he said, "Then come here."

She climbed over the shift, practically landing in his lap. She finally got settled in his arms. "I'm here."

"So you are," he said raggedly.

Then he kissed her, setting her world on fire. Delaney melted against him, trailing her hands inside his shirt. The hairs on his chest prickled sensuously against her palm. She wanted desperately to throw off her clothes and let him make love to her. She wanted to feel him naked, pressed against her, his body hard with need.

"Oh, Lord, Delaney," Lloyd moaned.

She swayed against him, reluctant to break their embrace. Lloyd kissed her again, drinking deeply of her lips, his tongue quickly invading her mouth. With a harsh intake of breath he slid his hands down her back to cup her buttocks, pulling her against him.

Then he pulled away just as abruptly, letting his breath out all at once.

"Is something wrong?" Delaney asked.

"No," he said, "not really. Things are just going along too fast for me."

Not realizing how aroused he was, and wanting only to kiss him again, she stroked her hands lovingly through his hair. "Lloyd, you once said I wasn't the lovers' lane type. What type am I?"

"You're not doing too bad here, Delaney."

"You know what I mean."

"Yes, I do know what you mean," he said, tracing

his finger along the neckline of her blouse. "You're the silk and satin type. Champagne. An expensive hotel, a night on the town."

"Actually this is kind of fun."

"For you, maybe," he said. "I don't know how much more of this I can take."

She chuckled huskily and took his hand from her collar to place it against her breast. "Come here, Captain Thomas."

"Lord," he murmured, trailing kisses along her cheek to her throat, then along the neckline of her blouse. Breathing deeply, he inhaled the sweet scent of her, his lips tasting and tantalizing her skin. "Give me strength."

"Oh, Lloyd," she said, running her hands over his arms, delighting in the hard, corded muscles that held her so tight. She heard an unexpected click in the background, but she merely arched against him, lost in the sensation of his touch.

Instead of strength, Lloyd should have asked for privacy, Delaney thought a few minutes later when the car door was abruptly pulled open. They nearly tumbled out.

Lloyd muttered an expletive as a bright light flashed in their eyes.

"What's going on in here?" a burly cop asked. "Things look awfully hot and heavy in this car."

Lloyd mumbled an expletive. "I forgot about patrols. I guess some things never change."

Delaney was mortified. She jerked her blouse straight and pulled her skirt down over her knees.

"You got it buddy," the policeman said. "Step outside the car."

"Excuse me, Officer—"

"How old are you, pal?" the cop interrupted, frowning and shining the light directly in Lloyd's face. Then he flicked it toward Delaney. "And how old is she? Oh," he said after a moment, "I guess she's old enough to know better."

Delaney glared at him.

"Officer—" Lloyd began.

"Why don't you two find a more appropriate spot for what you're doing?" the man went on. "This here's a lovers' lane. It's for kids."

"Yes, sir, Officer," Lloyd answered. "Sorry."

The man slammed the door closed. "Get the hell out of here."

As Lloyd started the car and they pulled away, Delaney couldn't help laughing. Most of the other cars were leaving, too. Apparently the police had blitzed the place. "I can't believe we got caught."

Lloyd laughed, too. "I can't believe we went there in the first place." He shook his head. "The man's right. That place is for kids. I'm thirty-eight years old."

She smiled and rested a hand on his thigh. She could feel him jump just from that slight contact. "We're almost home."

He turned to her slowly. "What did you say?"

His voice was hoarse and he was staring at her with undisguised passion. "You're having a hard time hearing me tonight, Lloyd. I said, we're almost home."

"And?"

"And I think the policeman was right. There are more appropriate places for what we were doing."

"Such as?"

"My bedroom."

Now that she had actually murmured the words, Delaney wondered if she would be able to go through with it. But she wanted him. There was no doubt about that. And she was ready to trust again—or at least to try.

Lloyd didn't say anything more and neither did Delaney. He took her hand as they got out of the car and went up her walk. Still silent, she unlocked her front door. They went inside.

Lloyd clicked the door closed behind them. The silence of the room seemed so loud it could have been a gunshot. But Delaney turned to him. She was a woman and she had made a decision; she wasn't going to back out now.

"Delaney," he said. "I—"

She placed her fingers over his lips. "Shh. Don't say it. Just kiss me."

With a groan he pulled her close. As his lips met hers, she moaned, too, from need, from longing, from gladness. For so long now she had wanted to give herself to him—completely, totally, and at last, this was the moment. She wanted him desperately.

"Hurry," she murmured. Now that she had made the decision she couldn't bear to wait a second longer. She wanted to tear off her clothes and feel him naked against her. She wanted him to take her now, this moment. "Please hurry, Lloyd."

"Delaney," he murmured, trailing a torrid path across her cheek and down her throat. "Delaney, a few more moments, and I won't be able to stop."

"Good. I don't want you to stop," she said. "I don't want you to ever stop."

"Are you sure? I want to make love to you, Delaney, but I need to know . . . are you sure you want that, too?"

"Yes. Oh, yes." She pressed against him, trying to show him how much she wanted him. "Yes, I'm certain I want you, Lloyd. I want you so much. Please . . . please make love to me."

Without further hesitation, Lloyd picked her up and carried her into the bedroom. After closing the door behind them, he gathered her close, crushing her against his length. Delaney didn't have the slightest idea how her blouse got unbuttoned, yet suddenly his dark head was bent between the tops of her breasts, which rose above her bra. Then the restraining garment was off, the straps falling over her shoulders in one quick movement. Her naked breasts surged in his hands. As his tongue flicked across her heated flesh, she thought she would surely die from the intense need that rushed through her body with each beat of her heart. A fiery glow flickered deep inside, flowing through her limbs, and she held him tightly.

"Delaney," he said hotly. "Oh, God, Delaney."

Then, pausing only to remove the rest of their clothes, he began a sensuous assault on her body, touching her, kissing her, caressing her. Thrilling to his touch, Delaney pressed against him, naked flesh to naked flesh. The hot, turgid evidence of his arousal felt like fire against her thighs.

They fell together across the bed. Lloyd made love to her gently, slowly, his lips and hands bringing her to the pinnacle of pleasure and back so many times that she wanted to cry out in frustration. All she could think of was the sensation of him possessing her, of feeling him inside her.

"Lloyd," she moaned, "please love me. Love me now."

"Only a moment more," he murmured.

"I can't stand it."

"We've waited a long time for this, Delaney. Let's not hurry now."

When he kissed her again, she moaned, reaching for him, needing him. His hands on her flesh, caressing and seeking, increased her fervor, and she arched toward him. His lips followed the path of his hands, leaving not an inch of her body untouched. Consumed with desire, Delaney felt as if a storm had swept through her, leaving her ravaged on the shore. But he didn't stop there; Lloyd discovered every secret place and tortured her with his touch, his lips, his mouth.

"Lloyd!" she cried, "Lloyd, please! I can't wait any longer."

"Oh, Lord, Delaney. I need you so."

With one slow, deep thrust he joined his body with hers, and she gasped aloud with pleasure. He paused a moment, keeping his eyes locked with hers in silent communion, then began to move inside her with long, piercing thrusts that came faster and faster. The white-hot fire blazed inside her, until together they touched the very core of the flames in a burst of ecstasy that left her breathless with wonder. Slowly, ever so slowly, the fire burned down to softly glowing embers. Languid from lingering warmth, Delaney was content, lying in Lloyd's arms.

"You are beautiful, Delaney," Lloyd said afterward, gathering her close and pushing her hair back from her sweat-dampened forehead. "So very beautiful."

The depth of her emotions overwhelmed her and tears brimmed in her eyes. Feeling foolish, she turned away.

Placing his hands on her shoulders, he forced her to face him. He kissed away the moisture. "Is something wrong, Delaney? Wasn't it good for you?"

"Oh, Lloyd." Now tears started streaming down her cheeks. She felt utterly ridiculous. Their lovemaking had been so wonderful. Why couldn't she tell him? "Lloyd, I'm sorry."

"For what? Tell me, Delaney. Tell me what's wrong?"

"I'm sorry for crying."

"That's all?"

"Yes."

"You're sure?"

She nodded. "Yes, that's all."

"Oh, love, that's crazy."

"I know. I can't help it."

"Come here." He held out his arms.

Still sniffling, Delaney buried her face in his chest as he held her close. She wanted to lie there forever, wrapped in his strong, protective arms.

But Lloyd started to caress her again, at first gently, brushing his lips across her forehead and eyelids. Then, as passion flared once more, he found her mouth in a harsh and demanding kiss. The embers stirred quickly inside Delaney, hot and bright. Eagerly, she drew his hands to her breasts. She gasped as his hands roved across her body, his breath hot and harsh against her skin. When his fingers stroked her stomach and the mound of silky hairs, she opened herself willingly to his touch.

"Delaney, this time it will be for you."

When he arched above her, she cried out, meeting his thrusting body time and time again. Filled with a deep, inexplicable joy, Delaney cried out as they braved the torrid wildfire. At the height of the blaze, Lloyd cried out, too, and collapsed beside her.

Chapter 8

LLOYD STAYED WITH her that night. And the next.
And the night after that. The days passed quickly,
and Delaney felt herself come alive as their whirlwind pace continued. Sometimes Curt would join
them for an excursion or a meal; sometimes they
would ask Mr. Peterson and his friend to come
along. Or Jean and her family would invite them
over, and they would chat over dessert and coffee,
mostly about Kevin, since Adrienne had taken a new
interest in her son. Now that the letters had started,
Delaney heard from Kevin every few days. He
seemed to be adjusting well, and was actually enjoying the life of a Marine.

Delaney was adjusting, too, to life without the son

who had been the center of her life for so many years. And Lloyd had become an integral part of her life. Sometimes it frightened her to realize how much she depended on him now, and how much she loved him. She couldn't quite admit that, though, not even to herself. For she was still haunted by the familiar feeling that something would happen to destroy her happiness.

Jean thought her fears were foolish—especially her concern for Curt, who was getting ready to leave for Marine training camp. Summer school had just ended, and the air now carried the nip of September. In a few short weeks he would be leaving.

"Why are you upset?" Jean asked. The two women were at the shop and had been talking for hours, between customers. "He's not even your kid, and he wants to go. He's looking forward to it. Besides, Kevin's doing great."

"I know," Delaney answered. "It just reminds me of when Kevin left." The two boys were vastly different on the surface. Kevin was so responsible, while Curt was more rebellious. Yet in his own way, Curt was a sensitive boy, and although she knew in her heart that the Marines would be good for him, Delaney still felt protective of the boy. "I've gotten attached to Curt."

"You'd get attached to a bumblebee if it needed love."

"I can't help it, Jean. I like kids."

"You should have had a pack of them. That would have cured you. Speaking of kids, when are you and Lloyd going to tie the knot and have a houseful?"

That was the last subject Delaney wanted to discuss. So far she'd managed to avoid the issue completely, and the man was as patient as a saint. She knew he loved her. He had shown it in so many ways. But she still wasn't ready. She needed just a little more time.

"Lloyd and I aren't ready to settle down."

Jean was hard to put off. "You'd think you were a couple of teenagers—'ready to settle down.' And even if that's a valid excuse for you, let me tell you, Delaney Anderson, that Captain Lloyd Thomas *is* ready to settle down. He's dying to marry you."

"He hasn't mentioned it to me."

"That's because he's a nice guy and he doesn't want to push you."

Delaney turned to her friend. "Have you and Lloyd been talking about me? Has he told you these things?"

"Of course he hasn't told me these things," Jean answered.

"Then how do you know he wants to marry me?"

"Oh, come on, Delaney, give me a little credit for all these years of observation. It's easy to see the man's head over heels in love with you. If you had any brains in your head at all you'd grab him and run. Are you waiting for disaster to strike? The man's a recruiter. Nothing's going to happen to him. You don't have to be afraid to love him, Delaney."

Jean knew her too well, Delaney decided. She *was* waiting for disaster to strike; and she was afraid to take the risk just in case it did. Delaney turned away. "Kevin said to tell Adrienne to write. How is she?"

"You're just trying to change the subject," Jean said, shaking her head.

Delaney smiled. "True."

"You know something, Delaney? Even if you can't admit you love Lloyd now, you know it would be a shame to lose him just because you're afraid to take a risk."

Delaney pulled a file out of the cabinet. "Have you told Mrs. Sullivan to pick up her bookmarks? They're done."

Jean sighed. "No."

"I'll call her right now."

When Delaney got home that night, Lloyd was almost finished trimming the hedge that grew along her property line. Although it was still hot out, the nights were cool and the leaves were starting to turn pale yellow. Lloyd wore jeans and the T-shirt that bore the Marine emblem. The noise of the trimmer was so loud that he hadn't heard her pull up. Delaney saw Lloyd put down the tool and dunk his head under the hose. Quietly, she got out of her car and took several steps toward him.

Sensing her presence, he dropped the hose and wheeled abruptly, nearly knocking her off her feet. She had forgotten about his Marine Corps split-second reflexes for a moment.

Lloyd grabbed her around the waist and smiled. "Delaney. Hello."

"Hi." Righting herself and regaining her balance, she smiled back. "Hard at work, huh?"

"Endless chore, your lawn."

"Where's Curt?"

"You know teenagers. He took a hike. You can count on him being back in time for dinner, though." Lloyd flicked water out of his hair. "It's hot. Got anything cool to drink?"

"Water."

"I've already had water," he said. "What happened to that lemonade you used to serve me on the porch? And the cookies? I checked; the cookie jar is empty."

"I've got you in my clutches now," Delaney teased, nodding toward the neatly trimmed hedge. "I don't need to give you lemonade and cookies." Actually she hadn't had much time to bake these days. They were always out doing things. "Besides, I don't want you developing a paunch."

"A paunch?" He patted his firm abdomen. "Delaney Anderson, I'll have you know I'm in perfect condition."

"Sure."

Delaney should have known better than to challenge Lloyd. "Feel," he commanded, taking her hand and slapping it on his abdomen. "That's steel, woman."

"Soft steel, maybe," she teased.

He leaned down to kiss her. "Slide your hand lower and say that," he murmured in her ear.

"Lloyd!" Delaney felt her face flame red.

He just laughed. "Ah, Delaney, you'll always blush." But he didn't move away. "Well?"

Handing him the hose, she stuck out her tongue. "Here. You need to cool off."

"And you," he countered, taking the hose and heading toward her, "need a lesson in diplomacy."

"Lloyd!" she said, suddenly realizing what he was about to do. "Lloyd, don't!"

"A man needs to be complimented, Delaney Anderson. A man needs his ego boosted. A man needs lemonade and cookies." He squirted her once, playfully.

"Lloyd!"

"What?"

She grabbed the hose and they struggled for control of it. By now, they were both soaking wet. Delaney fell to the ground, giggling helplessly. "I'll get you for this, Lloyd Thomas!"

He slipped and fell beside her, laughing too, and rolled on top of her. "Promises, promises. That's all I ever hear from you."

"You'll see." She tried to reach for the hose again, but he reversed their positions.

"Delaney, wait," he said. "Truce."

"Truce? Just when I'm winning!"

He smiled. "I've got a surprise for you."

They were in her front yard, rolling in the mud. Her skirt was probably hiked up above her waist, but she didn't care. "What surprise?"

Shifting slightly, he pulled a thin envelope from his jeans pocket and wiped it on his shirt before handing it to her. "They're a bit muddy but they'll still be good."

She frowned at Lloyd, still lying on top of him, as she opened the packet. What had he come up with now? Two tickets fell out. "Airline tickets?"

"To Charleston, South Carolina," he explained. "We can fly in and rent a car. I made reservations at Hilton Head Island. It's just across the way from Parris Island. I thought we could go to Kevin's graduation."

What a sweet gesture! Delaney didn't know what to say as emotion welled up in her throat. She had been avoiding this issue too; she had wanted to go, but couldn't seem to make the reservations. Lloyd was so thoughtful. "Are you sure you can get away?"

"I have one week's leave, just before Kevin's graduation. I thought we might swing up the coast and visit my folks."

"In North Carolina?"

He nodded. "They've been asking about you."

"Oh." The rest of Lloyd's proposal wasn't as simple as it sounded, and Delaney wasn't sure she was ready to meet his parents yet.

"It's not a bad drive," he went on. "And the coast is pretty. We'd go through Myrtle Beach. We could spend a couple days there."

"What about Curt?"

"He'll be fine," Lloyd answered. "He'll be going out on maneuvers that weekend, so he'll only be alone for a few days."

"But isn't he leaving soon?"

Lloyd nodded. "The end of the month."

Still holding the tickets, Delaney frowned. "You don't have to go on maneuvers? I thought you were partners with Curt."

"We are partners," he said. "Hell, we're more than partners. I feel like the boy's my son. But what does that have to do with our trip?"

"Don't you want to be with Curt?"

"We're only going to be gone a week, Delaney. Curt and I will be spending plenty of time together later on." Now Lloyd was frowning. "I thought you'd be excited. Don't you want to go?"

She forced a smile. "I am excited."

"You sure don't look it."

"You look all right," Mr. Peterson said, coming up beside them suddenly. "Sorry to interrupt," the older man went on, "but you two have been lying there for so long I thought maybe you'd hit your heads or something. I see you're just lying there."

"Lloyd squirted me with the hose." Delaney scrambled up, flicking little spots of mud from her dress.

"Looks like fun," the old man said.

Lloyd got up, too, and shut off the hose. "It was. Thanks for checking on us. I thought I might come over and fix that leak on your roof, if you're not going anywhere."

"I'm right here."

Lloyd stood to follow the older man back across the street. Lloyd's generosity was truly overwhelming, Delaney thought. "See you in a bit, okay?" he said to her. "We'll talk."

She nodded and went inside the house. She was just scared, that was all. The idea of meeting his parents petrified her.

But she didn't tell Lloyd that a few hours later when he asked her about the trip again. "It sounds great, Lloyd," she said.

They were in the kitchen. Delaney was washing the dishes, and Lloyd was drying them. "Sure?"

"I'm just nervous about seeing Kevin," she said. "I don't know if I'll be able to keep from crying." That was certainly the truth.

"Don't worry, Delaney. Even mothers who don't cry very often are allowed to fall apart at boot camp graduation."

"I'm trying very hard to let go of Kevin."

He smiled. "You're doing a good job. You only send brownies twice a week now," he teased her.

She couldn't help laughing. "Lloyd, I didn't bake anything this week."

"I know." He gave her a quick peck on the nose. "All too well. And I think I love you, Delaney Anderson."

It was just an endearment, she told herself. He couldn't mean it. She didn't love him, either—not really, not yet. She loved being with him; she loved making love with him. But actually *loving* him was too dangerous. The storm was approaching—fast. She knew it, and she knew she didn't want to be hurt again.

The coastal North Carolina town Lloyd came from could almost be termed quaint. As they drove northeast along Route 17 in their rented car, Delaney was charmed by the Old World atmosphere of the place. There were tall trees with low-hanging Spanish moss, buildings that looked as though they had been designed in the eighteenth century, and beautiful flowers in bloom. They were definitely in the country. As they drove farther toward the outskirts of town, the roads turned to gravel and then dirt, and the neat houses became small farms.

"I'm surprised," Delaney said to Lloyd. "For some reason I never took you for a country boy."

"Appearances are deceiving," he replied. "I do have humble beginnings."

There was nothing wrong with that. Now he was a captain in the Marine Corps—no easy task—and he'd come up through the ranks. But Lloyd wouldn't apologize for his heritage; he was merely explaining it.

"Your folks never moved?"

"I couldn't drag them away from this place. They

both grew up here and they insist they're going to die here, too."

"That says something for the town."

"The economy's not so good, though. Dad grows tobacco, which you'd think would be pretty lucrative, but year after year he just barely makes a living."

"Not enough help?"

"Not enough land. And it's a very competitive market. Every year it comes down to that old devil, supply and demand. But my parents are pretty happy, and in the end, that's what counts."

"Did you help them farm tobacco?"

"Sure. I rolled it and smoked it, too."

They had pulled into a narrow driveway and came to a stop in front of a small white two-story house. A man and a woman were waiting on the front porch.

The man was tall, like Lloyd, with blond hair and striking blue eyes. His mother was small and dark. They were more friendly than anyone Delaney had ever met, hugging her and making her feel instantly welcome.

And instantly guilty. It became obvious over the next several days that they both assumed Lloyd and Delaney were serious. Mrs. Thomas kept hinting about marriage, and Lloyd, sensing Delaney's uneasiness with the subject, kept putting his mother off with a kiss or a joke.

But the next morning when Delaney came downstairs, Mrs. Thomas was in the kitchen alone.

"Coffee?" the woman called cheerfully.

"Please."

Delaney smiled at the huge piece of coffee cake Lloyd's mother placed beside her steaming mug.

Mothers were alike the world over, she thought, recognizing herself in Mrs. Thomas. Only this time Delaney had become the child. And she was actually enjoying the attention. Although she was close to her own mother, they had not lived near each other since Delaney had married. When Richard died, Delaney's mother had offered to move back to the Chicago area, but Delaney's stepfather enjoyed the Florida climate and she had not wanted them to sacrifice that for her. Now she realized what she had been missing.

"Lloydie's out with Dad," Mrs. Thomas said. "I thought we could have a little chat."

Lloydie? "What did you want to chat about?" she asked, already growing uncomfortable.

"Oh, nothing special. I just wanted to get to know you. Do you bake much?"

"Almost as much as you," Delaney answered. "But I must admit, my coffee cake isn't as good as yours."

The woman beamed. "Thank you."

"You'll have to tell me your secret."

"I grind my own cinnamon. I add just a little lemon juice."

"It's not at all crumbly," Delaney said, biting into the cake.

"It's the oil," the woman said.

They started discussing recipes, and suddenly Delaney realized Mrs. Thomas wasn't being at all intimidating. She was just a mother, like Delaney, worried about her son. She told Delaney about Lloyd's childhood and about his ex-wife, Amy. Delaney found herself opening up about her own losses in life.

Later, when Lloyd came in with Mr. Thomas, Delaney poured coffee for them all. Afterward, she hugged Mrs. Thomas. "Thanks," she said, "for making me feel like a member of your family."

"I hope you'll be part of my family soon," Mrs. Thomas answered.

Delaney just smiled.

They visited with Lloyd's parents for three days. On their last morning, Lloyd took Delaney out in a rowboat to Cape Fear. The Atlantic Ocean was cold and gray and forbidding. Lloyd handled the currents expertly, but waves still chopped over the tiny boat, and Delaney felt small and insignificant. How he could have done this as a child, in a storm, was beyond imagining.

Shipping the oars, he swept his arm out in an arc. "Great, isn't it?"

Delaney glanced all around her. "It's like the roller coaster, Lloyd. The best part will be when it's over."

He glanced at her, surprised. "Are you scared?"

"Not at all," she lied. "This is fun."

He laughed. "I won't make you come out again."

"No, but you might decide to soothe me."

He laughed again. "That's a good idea." He started to change his position. The boat pitched violently.

"Lloyd!"

He calmly sat on the narrow stern seat and put his arm around her.

"Oh, God," she said.

"Take a deep breath, Delaney."

She inhaled and exhaled several times.

"And open your eyes. How can you see the ocean with your eyes closed?"

"I don't want to see the ocean."

"But it's beautiful. Look, there's a fish. And the colors—it's green in some places, blue in others."

"It's gray."

"How do you know? Your eyes are still closed."

"Okay, they're open," she said, peeking out slightly. Breathing deeply helped. She felt less nauseated. Automatically she leaned into Lloyd's warmth, his strength.

"I'm beginning to think you're a sadist, Lloyd Thomas."

"Why's that? Because I make you look at the ocean?"

"No, because you bring me out here in the middle of the Atlantic Ocean in a rowboat and scare me to death by switching positions."

"That wasn't sadistic, Delaney. It was practical."

"I suppose you're going to explain that statement to me?"

"No," he said, "I'm going to demonstrate the truth of that statement."

She glanced up at him. "Pardon?"

"I've done everything there is to do on this ocean, except kiss you," he said huskily.

As his lips lowered to hers, Delaney's world started spinning again, only it wasn't the ocean that caused her dizziness. It was Lloyd—his touch, his kiss. For three days they had had to be content with brief embraces, glances across a room. Now, alone and in his arms, she wanted to be swept away on the tidal wave of his kiss.

When he pulled back, she murmured, "There's one other thing you haven't done on this ocean."

"What's that?" he said hoarsely.

"You haven't made love to me."

He cocked his head to one side and studied her for a moment. "I know where there's a secluded beach."

She smiled. "You're on. I'll help row."

He laughed, but he moved to the center seat and picked up the oars. When they came ashore, they made love in the sand with the surf pounding at their heels. At the height of their love, Delaney thought surely she would die from the depth of her emotions.

They left North Carolina that afternoon and headed down the coast toward Parris Island. They decided to skip Myrtle Beach, since Delaney was anxious to see Kevin. Late that night they pulled into a parking lot on Hilton Head Island. They had slept separately at Lloyd's parents' home, and Delaney had assumed Lloyd would get them a double room. Instead, he came back to the car with two keys.

"I hope you don't mind, I got us a two-bedroom villa," he said, handing her one of the keys. "You don't have to unlock your bedroom door unless you want to. And you certainly don't have to unlock it tonight," he went on, leaning over to give her one of his quick kisses. "You look exhausted."

How could he be so concerned about propriety after what they had shared on the beach? "I think the Atlantic was my Waterloo," she said.

Apparently recalling their lovemaking, he grinned. "I'm glad I could be the conquerer."

She made a face, but was too tired to come up with a sharp retort. She scarcely glanced at the comfortable sitting room, or the large, lovely bedroom with a panoramic view of the ocean. As soon as Lloyd brought their luggage up and set hers in her room, she said, "I'm too tired to unlock the door, but don't bother going to your room. We can both sleep here."

"Sure? There's only one bed." He was teasing, but his voice was full of concern.

She glanced at the huge bed and then at him, her hands on her hips. "I think we can fit."

"Maybe," he agreed, "if we snuggle."

She smiled at him. "I'm a champ at snuggling."

Very early the next morning, snuggling led to other things. A touch became a caress, a kiss became a deep embrace. Lloyd made love to her in the big, sprawling bed.

Afterward he drew her close. "I've missed you, Delaney," he murmured, his lips against her forehead. "I've missed holding you in my arms."

"I've missed you, too, Lloyd." And she had, more than she would have thought possible. Perhaps Jean was right—Lloyd had already become a part of her life. If she had to lose him, it would be even more painful than she'd thought. But she shook off her gloomy thoughts. They would see Kevin today. "We should take a shower."

"Mmm," he agreed. "Want to take one together?"

"Yes," she said, "but we'll never get anywhere if we do."

"You're right," he said, slapping her bare behind affectionately. "You go first."

"Ouch!" Delaney nearly jumped from the bed and shot him a scathing look. "I can see why you're a captain. You're great at giving orders."

"Wait'll you meet Kevin's drill instructor. The Marines import them from Camp Mean."

She stalked off toward the shower. "I think you missed your calling."

The Marine Corps Recruit Depot at Parris Island brought back memories of places Delaney had lived, both as a child and as the wife of a Navy man. They entered through the main gates and drove first to the visitors' center and public affairs office, located at the heart of the base. Individual barracks marked the boundaries of a vast expanse of parade grounds where recruits learned to march. Other buildings— the exchange, a laundry depot, a theater, the officers' quarters, and a small fire house and gas station— were clustered near the visitors' center.

Lloyd pointed out the landmarks as they got out of the car and stepped inside one of the buildings to check in with a friend of his. "The rifle range is over there, near the obstacle course. There are a couple of other training areas as well, and some large fields for maneuvers."

By now Delaney was anxious to see Kevin. What would he look like? "There's an Iwo Jima monument here, isn't there?" She tried not to let her nervousness show.

"We passed it on the way in. It's near the recruits' chapel."

"Oh." Delaney hadn't even noticed the memorial; she had been watching for Kevin, thinking she might spot him in the crowds of people milling about the base. Military bases were like small cities; people were everywhere, and she knew it was unlikely that she'd see Kevin by accident.

Lloyd steered her through one door and knocked on another, nodding to people he knew along the way. No one asked him who he was; the captain's bars on his uniform spoke louder than words. "Kevin's unit is scheduled to go out on maneuvers today."

Delaney frowned. "Then why are we here?"

"You'll see."

A few moments later, a door opened and her son stood in the entrance, smiling down at her. "Hi, Mom. Captain Thomas."

"Kevin!" Tears sprang into her eyes. "Oh, Kevin."

He laughed and hugged her close. "It's good to see you, Mom."

Delaney couldn't stop crying. She hugged him for several long moments. Finally she pulled back. Lloyd handed her a handkerchief and she dabbed at her eyes.

"Good to see you, too, Captain," Kevin said. "Thanks for bringing my mom."

"My pleasure."

"Thanks for taking care of her, too, these past few weeks. I hear you two have been getting along pretty good."

That was certainly an understatement, Delaney thought.

"That's also been my pleasure," Lloyd answered.

Delaney just hugged Kevin again. "Let me look at you."

"I haven't changed much," he said. "It's only been ten weeks."

It seemed like a lifetime. Kevin was dressed in a khaki and green outfit similar to the one Lloyd sometimes wore, and he held a garrison cap. He seemed taller than she remembered, and stronger; the angle of his jaw was proud. "Your hair's still short."

He gave a half-laugh and rubbed his hand across his head. "Yeah, feels funny. It's growing back."

"It looks great," Delaney said. "You look great." She glanced at Lloyd in confusion, then back at Kevin. "Don't you have maneuvers today?"

"No, I've got a short leave today. Lloyd just wanted to surprise you."

"So you're responsible for this." Delaney looked at Lloyd and felt a deep tenderness.

Kevin nodded. "Lloyd called my C.O. last week. Want to see the base?" he went on as Delaney flashed Lloyd a grateful smile. "I thought we could take a little tour."

Delaney had seen hundreds of military bases. "Wouldn't you rather go into town?"

"I'm kind of proud of the base. I'd like to show you around, if you don't mind."

"I'd love to see it," Delaney said.

Kevin opened the door for them. As they went out, Delaney grasped Lloyd's hand. "Thanks," she murmured to him.

He squeezed her hand tightly in response and smiled. "It was no trouble, Delaney."

Kevin had truly grown up, Delaney realized as he proudly pointed out buildings and told them about his experiences. He had become a man, and although she would always be his mother, he really didn't need her anymore. They had separate identities now, and he would have to make his own way in the world, start his own family, have his own adventures.

"Tell me about your drill instructor," she said. "Is he pretty mean?"

Kevin laughed. "You bet. Boot camp's been tough. I don't regret a single moment, but I'd never want to go through it again."

"I'm proud of you, Kevin."

He smiled at Lloyd, and then at her. "I'm proud of you, too, Mom." This time their hug meant more than the love between a mother and son.

A few hours later Kevin had to be back on duty. Promising to see him the next evening, Delaney and Lloyd went back to the resort on Hilton Head Island. Graduation was in two more days.

"I'm proud of you, too, Delaney," Lloyd said as they pulled onto the highway.

"I guess I've grown up," she said, and laughed quietly.

"You've changed," Lloyd agreed.

"For the better?"

He nodded. "Definitely for the better." There was a brief silence. "Anything special you want to do?"

She shrugged. "I don't know. What do you have in mind?" At his leer, she amended, "Any special activity?"

He just laughed. "Okay, a special activity. You're not very good at miniature golf, as I recall, but how about regular golf? They've got a fantastic course here."

"I'm lousy at it," Delaney answered.

"Horseback riding?"

She glared at him. "All I did last time was bounce."

"It was an attractive bounce."

"Lloyd," she drew out his name.

"Okay, no horseback riding today. We'll do it another day, though. There's nothing like riding alongside the ocean."

"I see you have a fetish for oceans, too."

"Water," he agreed. "Any kind of water."

"Well, what do you say we just lie by the pool, then? That looked pretty fantastic, too."

He grinned. "Sure thing. The pool it is."

They went swimming and, later on, ate dinner in a nearby restaurant. For most of the afternoon Delaney had been wondering how she could thank Lloyd for his thoughtfulness and show him how much he meant to her. Seeing Kevin here had helped her to accept the fact that he was a soldier. And she had come to understand that the storm could hit at any time. It wasn't worth living in fear if there was someone you cared about to fight for instead.

Now she knew she truly cared. They were in the cocktail lounge after dinner, dancing. She glanced up at Lloyd. He wasn't just everybody's hero; he was her hero. "Why don't you order a drink and meet me in our room in half an hour," she said softly.

He looked puzzled, but said nothing.

She gave him a quick kiss and smiled mysteriously. "And make sure you give me the entire half-hour."

"Delaney, what are you up to?" He frowned as she pulled away. "Where are you going?"

"To our room," she said. "I've got a surprise for you, Captain Lloyd Thomas." Passing by a waiter, she took two glasses and a bottle of champagne from his tray, knowing Lloyd would sign for it.

The moment Delaney got to the room, she called

the front desk. "I need a dozen roses, several candles, and satin sheets. Immediately, please."

"Satin sheets?"

"Don't you have a honeymoon suite?"

"No, ma'am."

Delaney chewed her lip. She wanted this surprise to be special. "How about a gift shop? You can buy the sheets and put them on my bill."

"Yes, we have a gift shop. I don't know if they carry satin sheets or not, though. It's an unusual item."

"It's very important," Delaney said firmly. "Please try. And there's a man in the bar. A gorgeous man in a Marine uniform. Don't let him come up until you get the sheets."

"I see. We'll do our best, Mrs. Anderson," the man said.

Delaney thanked him and hung up.

Half an hour later she had showered and perfumed her entire body. She tossed on her robe and answered the door. A maid stood there, her arms loaded with candles, roses, and satin sheets. She handed them to Delaney. "Will that be all, ma'am?"

Delaney smiled. "Yes, thank you."

"We had to search through our linen rooms for the sheets," the woman explained.

"I'll make it worth your while."

The maid nodded. She turned, as if to leave, then seemed to remember something. Turning to Delaney, she said, "Captain Thomas would like to know if he may now come upstairs."

"Ask him to wait five more minutes," Delaney said.

Delaney tipped the woman generously and closed

the door. She pulled the petals from the red roses and spread them out over the white satin sheets. After turning the radio on to a station with some soft music, she lit the candles and placed them all around the room. She had just finished when Lloyd knocked.

"Delaney, can I come in?"

Taking off her robe, she lay down on the bed in what she hoped was a seductive pose, pulling the top sheet up to just below her breasts. She let her long hair fall over them. Lord, she hoped she didn't merely look foolish. "Come in, Lloyd."

The expression on his face made all her efforts worthwhile. For a moment he just stared at her. "Delaney?" he said finally. "I—uh—what is this?"

"Don't you like my surprise?"

"I'm—" He cleared his throat. "Oh, yes, I like your surprise."

"Do I look all right?"

"All right?" He nearly choked. "You're beautiful, Delaney."

"There's satin sheets, champagne."

"I see," he said as he walked toward her. "What's the occasion?"

She held out her arms to him. "Lloyd Thomas, I think I love you."

Chapter 9

DELANEY WASN'T AWARE of the exact moment when she ceased to think rationally; she was completely swept up in the wild, sweet force of their passion. She only knew that she responded eagerly to Lloyd's caresses, matching each one with her own, letting him know with her touch how deeply she cared for him.

When Lloyd possessed her, she thought she would explode from the intense shuddering of her body. It was the sweetest moment of her life. Thousands of stars shattered around her, and her world whirled with a dizzying force as he stroked her to a quivering peak, then brought her over the tumult of pleasure into a sea of tranquillity. Tears of joy slipped from her closed eyes. The union of their bodies transcended anything she had ever known. She felt as if they were a single being, two souls melded into one.

Afterward, she lay against his chest. He smoothed back her damp hair and kissed her. "Thank you, Delaney," he murmured.

She glanced up at him. "For what?"

"For a very special night. For your love. I love you, Delaney Anderson, more than I ever thought humanly possible."

"And I love you, Lloyd."

Then, with the sound of the ocean outside, he started to stroke her breasts again.

The next morning Delaney stretched luxuriously in the big bed, feeling deliciously tired. Lloyd rolled over, too, and took her in his arms.

" 'Morning," he said.

"Mmmm," she answered as he kissed her. "Good morning."

"Sleep well?"

"I hardly slept at all." She laughed and returned his kiss. "Thanks to you."

"Are you complaining?"

"Maybe a little," she admitted, realizing that a few of her muscles were actually sore. "I don't think I'm up to many of these kinds of nights."

"So, finally going to admit you're an old lady?"

"Absolutely not!" she said. "I'm just a woman who needs her rest."

"Ah, yes, beauty rest. But, Delaney, they say there's no rest for the wicked."

"And just what do you mean by that?" She glared at him with mock indignation.

"Look at this place." He gestured around the room at the candles, now burned low, the empty champagne bottle, and the sheets, strewn with rose petals. "It's positively decadent." Then he turned his gaze on her and let his hand trail lightly across her breasts, down her abdomen. "You're a wanton woman, Delaney Anderson. I'll have you know that none of this was my idea."

"It was mine. All mine," she said smugly, moving closer to him, trying to entice him. Weeks ago she wouldn't have dreamed of being so bold. "And I'm all yours."

Sighing, he lifted the sheet and tucked it under her chin. "I think we should talk."

He seemed so serious all of a sudden. What could possibly be bothering him? She tucked the pillow under her head. "Sure. What about?"

"Us. Our future together." He took a deep breath. For the first time since she had met him, he seemed nervous. "You know being in the Marines is my life. It's all I've ever known, Delaney. The military has given me so much. It's all I've ever done."

"I know," she said, nodding slowly. What was he getting at?"

"But I know how you feel about the service," he went on. "I realize you have a right to be bitter, so I thought we should talk about how that might affect us."

"Okay," she said softly, waiting for him to continue. She had already accepted the fact that he was a Marine and that she loved him.

"Before I went on leave, I was offered a fairly attractive package . . . if I reenlist."

"I thought you had a year left on your last reenlistment. Didn't you say you'd already served nineteen years?"

"I do have a year left, but early reenlistment isn't unusual, particularly for people of my rank. They've offered me a lucrative package, along with a signing bonus. And I'll probably be promoted to the rank of major."

Delaney knew that would be important to Lloyd. "Would you be reassigned to a new location?"

"Maybe." He nodded. "There's always that possibility. I am a soldier. There are never any guarantees."

"Where would you have to go?"

"I don't know." He hesitated a moment, seeming nervous again. "But wherever it is, I'd like you to go with me."

She swallowed the lump of tension in her throat. She hadn't even realized she'd been waiting anxiously for him to get to the point.

"I know it would be hard for you, but we wouldn't have to live on a base. We could always get a house in town. And as a major I would get more benefits."

"Lloyd . . ." Delaney moistened her lips. Did she have the courage to ask?

"You'd have full medical benefits, of course. And the commissary for shopping, and—"

"Lloyd," she interrupted, "are you asking me to live with you?"

He sighed, raking a hand through his hair. "I'm asking you to marry me, Delaney," he finally said. "Will you?"

"Yes."

"Yes?" He looked surprised. "Did you say yes?"

She smiled. "Yes."

"That's all?"

"Yes. Yes, yes, yes." Answers were simple when you were sure. "What do you want me to say?"

"How about when?"

"Okay, when?"

"As soon as we can make the arrangements."

"Yes."

He still looked anxious, as though he couldn't believe what he was hearing. "What about the Marines?"

She took his hands in hers. It was odd to see him less than self-assured. "The Marines are part of you, Lloyd. I know that. I can accept it."

He pulled her close, letting his breath out all at once in a sigh of relief. "Thank you, Delaney."

"You don't have to thank me, Lloyd," she murmured. "I love you."

"I love you, too. God, how I love you." He kissed her. Then he groaned and murmured against her lips, "You know, Delaney, if we keep this up we're never going to make it out of bed."

She laughed and arched against him. "I know."

Groaning again, Lloyd pulled away. "We need to finish talking first."

"You know, Lloyd," she teased, tiptoeing her fingers down his chest and abdomen, "they say that actions speak louder than words."

"But words are the tools of civilization."

"Goodness, you're a hard man to tempt."

"I'm a Marine."

"What about all those years of tradition?"

"After we talk."

She sighed regretfully. "Back to that, huh?"

"It's important."

The way he said it made her realize it *was* important. "I'm sorry, Lloyd."

"Well, it's not *that* important," he said. "I like you unserious, Delaney, so don't apologize. I was just wondering about Kevin. How do you think he'll react?"

"Kevin worships you," Delaney answered. "I think he'll be delighted."

"Even if we present him with a baby brother or sister?"

Delaney was touched. She hadn't really thought that far ahead; she certainly didn't think Kevin would object. "Tell you what, we won't give him a choice."

"Is that how you handle your kids?"

"It's the only way."

"I think I like your attitude." Slowly Lloyd started to pull the sheet down. "Maybe we should start working on our baby now, so we can break the news right away."

"I thought we had to finish talking."

"We did."

"I thought we had to go horseback riding."

He pulled the sheet lower. His gaze was hot on her body. "We do."

They never made it to the trails that morning, or that afternoon, but Lloyd and Delaney stayed at the Hilton Head Island resort for two more days. They swam, played golf, and just lay in the sun, relaxing. They went for long walks along the beach, letting the surf and the sand sift over their feet. In the evenings they visited with Kevin. As Delaney had suspected, Kevin was delighted with their news, and immediately wished them both congratulations. After his graduation, on the third day, Delaney and Lloyd flew home. Kevin had a two-week leave, but was flying on standby a few days later.

O'Hare Airport was crowded when Lloyd and Delaney arrived back home. Although it was Sunday, the terminals were packed. When they'd left for Parris Island, Lloyd had parked his El Camino at the airport and after waiting for their luggage they found the car and headed home. Traffic on the expressway was bad, but Lloyd handled the car well. She glanced at his strong profile, at his hands on the wheel. Even in the darkness of the car, he had an aura of strength, of command.

"We'll be home soon," he said, as though sensing her uneasiness. "The turnoff's just ahead."

She nodded. "It'll be good to get home."

"Did you have a good time?"

"Yes."

"Come closer." He patted the seat beside him.

She glanced around at the other cars. "We'll look like a couple of teenagers."

"What's so bad about that?" Lloyd flashed a smile. "Sometimes teenagers have good ideas."

"True," Delaney agreed, moving closer to him.

"What do you want to do tomorrow?"

She leaned her head on his shoulder. "Rest."

He laughed. "You had a week of rest."

"Maybe it's jet lag."

"I thought jet lag happens when you travel through several time zones."

"Maybe it's my age," she teased. "I am thirty-four, remember."

"Of course I remember."

"Tonight I seem to be feeling every year."

"You're almost thirty-five," he said.

She lifted her head. "How did you know that?"

"Kevin told me. He's got a big surprise planned for your birthday, and he didn't want me to miss it."

"I can imagine," Delaney said. "Don't even give me a hint. I don't want to think about it."

Lloyd laughed. "Thirty-five isn't so bad, Delaney. I'm close to forty, sweetheart. Anyhow, getting back to jet lag. I thought we might head for Florida right away to visit your mother and stepfather."

"I'm afraid that will have to wait a few weeks," Delaney said. "They're in Mexico."

He frowned at her. "When did they go to Mexico?"

"Last week. Didn't I show you the letter?"

"Are you sure you want me to meet them?"

For the second time she heard insecurity in his voice. She smiled at him. "I love you, Lloyd Thomas." Those words were easier and easier to say. "And yes, I want you to meet my parents. Very much. We'll go as soon as they get back."

"I'll put in for leave. Do you have any special plans for later on this week when Kevin comes home? I can ask for a couple of days then, too."

They had finally pulled into her driveway. "No— just a lot of home cooking, which is probably all he will want. I have a feeling he's going to be seeing quite a bit of Adrienne in the next two weeks. They've been writing to each other."

"That's good. It'll give us more time alone."

She glanced at him. "Were you worried?"

"Delaney, it's not always easy to court a mother when her son is around."

"No, I guess not. Especially a teenager—they tend to stay up late."

"Too late," Lloyd added with a sly grin.

He took Delaney's luggage out of his car and walked her to the door. They had already decided that he would go back to his own apartment to catch up on some paperwork.

She got out her keys. "Would you like to come in for coffee?"

"Maybe just one cup," he said. "I'm tired, too. I have to be on duty in the morning, and I've got all those forms waiting for me."

Delaney had just measured out the coffee grounds when the doorbell rang. "I'll get it," Lloyd called, going to the door. "It's probably Fred."

Mr. Peterson had been taking in her mail, and Delaney went to the door, too, to thank him. They had bought him a souvenir. "Lloyd, where's that shell?"

"In your suitcase, I think," he called over his shoulder. "Do you want me to get it?"

"Sure." But it wasn't Mr. Peterson at the door. Delaney recognized Sergeant Kendall, one of the soldiers who worked at the recruiting station. The moment she saw him Delaney knew something was wrong. She could tell by the man's stance, the nuances of his body language, and she stood completely still, knowing what would happen next. She'd been through this twice: the knock on the door, the soft words that skirted the issue at first. Then the announcement. Was it Kevin this time?

Oh, God, no. Let it be something else. They had just seen her son, and he was fine. He had just become a man.

But the soldier addressed Lloyd. "I'm glad you're

here, sir," he said. "I was hoping your flight would get in on time. I went to your apartment first."

Lloyd frowned. "Is something wrong?"

The man nodded. "Yes, sir. There's been an accident."

"An accident?" Lloyd repeated slowly.

The man explained. "There was an explosion up at the camp. I'm afraid there were a few fatalities among the boys we're recruiting."

Lloyd looked stunned. "What happened?"

"We don't know any of the details yet, sir," the man said. "We're not sure exactly how many men were killed. Medical teams and choppers were sent in, but communications are still poor. We do know that the fire is still very intense." He shrugged; it was a gesture of frustration, of helplessness. "The fire fighters think it may have been a natural gas pocket that got hit by one of the flame throwers, sir."

"The recruits were using flame throwers?"

"They were at the range, with all the proper precautions. The man who radioed us the news said that all of a sudden it seemed like the ground just exploded. Then there was a series of smaller explosions. He said it looked like there was a ring of fire around the camp."

It was an accident, something that couldn't have been prevented, Delaney thought. But that didn't make it seem any less terrible.

"When did this happen?" Lloyd asked.

"A couple of hours ago."

"Where were the troops?"

"Right in the middle."

Lloyd stared at the man in the doorway for a long moment. "Was Curt out this weekend?"

The sergeant nodded and said gently, "Yes, sir, he was. That's why I'm here."

Delaney had never seen a man turn totally white, as Lloyd did then. "Was he killed?"

"He's still missing. I'm sorry, sir. I know you were attached to the boy."

For a moment Lloyd slumped against the doorway. Delaney felt his anguish as sharply as she had felt her own all those years ago. How horrible! They both had loved Curt, and Lloyd was like a father to the boy. She took his hand and squeezed tightly, hoping he would feel her support. Lloyd quickly regained control, pulling his body erect as he took his hand from hers.

"I'll be right there," he said to the soldier. "We'll leave immediately." He turned to go inside the house and practically collided with Delaney, glancing at her as though he had just realized she was beside him. "God," he said, his voice ragged. "Curt's out there, Delaney. He's missing."

"I know," she said softly.

She wanted to take him in her arms and comfort him, but she knew he was trying to hold himself together. "Stay here," he said. "I'll be back as soon as I can get word."

"No, I'd rather come with you," she said.

Lloyd shook his head. "I don't know what the conditions are like out there. It's too dangerous."

"Please, Lloyd," she quietly. "Don't leave me here to worry about you both. Let me come with you."

"You're a civilian." He frowned. "I don't—"

"Mrs. Anderson can come, Captain Thomas, if you'd like," the soldier standing by the door told him. "They've got a command post set up away from the fire. No one will mind if she waits with you."

"I—" Lloyd frowned again.

Delaney could tell he was torn, not wanting her to get hurt. "I want to go," she said, taking his hand again. "Lloyd, we need to be together through this. We can help each other."

They reached the camp much sooner than Delaney would have thought possible. Sergeant Kendall drove and Lloyd and Delaney sat silently in the back seat of the official car, side by side, holding hands. She could tell Lloyd was distraught; the anguish on his face was plain for anyone to see.

The camp was located outside a small town near the Wisconsin state line. The area was heavily wooded, and they had watched the dark cloud of smoke for miles. When they got to the command post the camp looked like a wall of fire, crackling and popping as sparks flew through the sky. Weary, soot-strewn fire fighters rushed around with hoses, battling what seemed to Delaney to be a hopeless cause. Flames shot through the dry timber that surrounded the camp as men carried buckets of earth to smother embers that blew onto the grass from the tall trees.

Delaney knew Lloyd needed hope. She held his hand tightly. "Maybe Curt has made it out."

But she doubted that anyone could make it out of that inferno alive. Lloyd looked at her through pain-filled eyes. "Maybe."

Another officer met them at the car.

"Any word?" Lloyd asked him as soon as he had opened the door.

The officer shook his head. "Nothing. Sorry, sir."

Lloyd nodded. "What's being done?"

"We've got the fire fighters pretty well organized, we've re-established full communications, and we've called in some experts. If it is natural gas, we haven't got much hope of putting the fire out. At this point we're just trying to contain it. And now it's spread to the timber—everything here has been so dry. They haven't had much rain this way the past few weeks."

"What about the men still trapped inside the ring of fire?"

"If they survived the initial blast—" The man stopped abruptly, then murmured, "God, it was awful."

"What are the chances?" Lloyd asked.

The officer frowned. "Pretty slim. That whole area just blew up, one, two, three. But if any of the recruits did survive, we're hoping they crossed the river and got out on the other side before the fire surrounded them."

"Have you sent anyone to the other side to check?"

"Yes, sir."

"And?"

"Nothing. We have fire fighters posted all around the camp." The man shrugged. "Nothing anywhere."

"How many men were there?" Lloyd asked after a long moment.

"Fifteen, sir."

"When will we know?"

"I hope by tonight, at the latest."

"Have their families been notified?"

"Only the casualties. We did find two bodies that were thrown out of the fire ring."

Lloyd nodded again. "Good job, Markus."

"Thank you, sir."

Delaney realized then that Lloyd outranked the other officer, and that this was Lloyd's unit. Many of the men here were under his command. She also realized that all those trapped in the fire were boys he had recruited personally—Curt wasn't the only one. Now their chances for survival were bleak.

"If any of the relatives of the deceased call, please let me speak to them," Lloyd said after a moment.

"Yes, sir. There's coffee in the command post, sir."

Lloyd nodded. He started to pick up a bucket, but an officer in charge of the fire fighters stopped him. "With all due respect, sir," he said, "you'd be more help to us inside, keeping tabs on things."

"I need to do something."

"There's plenty to do inside."

They waited for hours. Several men were at the telephone; others filled out reports. Lloyd paced back and forth across the small room in the command post, glancing out the window at the flames every few minutes.

Delaney sat on a wooden bench, absently studying the map of the area, which someone had tacked to a bulletin board. The camp covered several hundred acres, mostly overgrown with timber for conducting simulated guerrilla warfare, with a river running through its center. Suspension bridges and ropes for swinging crisscrossed the water. And now the camp was surrounded by a wall of flames.

"Coffee, ma'am?" one of the soldiers waiting with them asked after another long hour had passed.

"Yes, thank you." She stood up. "I'll take some to Captain Thomas, too."

"I asked him, but he's kind of preoccupied."

"Maybe I can get through to him."

The soldier handed her two mugs of coffee. Delaney went to where Lloyd stood by the window. "Lloyd?" she called softly. "I've brought you coffee."

He turned to her, taking the cup from her hands automatically. "Thanks." Then he turned back to the window. "Peacetime," he said under his breath.

Delaney was surprised at the bitterness in his tone. Lloyd should realize that this accident had nothing to do with war or peace. In a way it had nothing to do with the military. The boys out there had simply been in the wrong place at the wrong time. "You can't blame yourself for this, Lloyd."

"No?"

"Didn't they say it was a natural gas pocket that caused the explosion?"

"Maybe."

"It was an accident, anyway. Something that no one could have predicted."

"Maybe, but Curt's out there because of me."

"Curt wanted to join the Marines."

Lloyd spun back to her. "You were right, you know, Delaney, that first day we met. I am all show, brass buttons, fancy uniform." He laughed harshly. "Tradition—"

"Lloyd, don't," she cut in. "Don't do this to yourself. I know how you feel but you can't blame yourself. This just isn't your fault."

He walked a few paces, then turned again to the window, shoving his hands deep in his pockets. He did not answer her.

"Lloyd, this fire is something no one could have foreseen," Delaney continued softly. "There was no way you could have prevented this."

He sighed, still staring out the window. "Those boys didn't have to be out there. Do you know *why* they were out there? Do you know why Curt was there?"

"Yes," she said, knowing he would tell her anyway.

"He's out there because of me. He signed up for the Marines because of me. Don't you understand, Delaney? This is the first time anyone has signed up directly because of me, because he wanted to be like me."

"That's not such a bad thing, Lloyd," she said.

"But it's a hell of a responsibility."

There was nothing she could say to him. When she went to him, wanting to comfort him, he slipped his hand in hers, but he wasn't really there. He was far away, living his own agony.

Finally one of the fire fighters came inside. Lloyd turned to him immediately. "Any progress?"

"We've got the fire contained, Captain Thomas," the man answered. "That's a plus. Give us a couple more hours."

"Can you call in another fire department?"

"More water won't help this fire, sir. It'll keep the timber from going up, but we've already got that under control. It's the gas we're worried about now."

"The gas is still burning?"

"Yes, sir."

"Can't you put dry chemicals on it?"

"That would be risky, sir. Some of the gas could dissipate in the air and cause another flash fire nearby. Then we'd set even more of the woods on fire and be right back where we started. Don't worry, Captain," the man went on. "As soon as the pocket's depleted, we can put the fire out completely and get in there to search for those boys."

"If there's anyone left to search for," Lloyd said, almost to himself. "God help them, I think they must be dead by now."

Delaney went to him then, and she held him close. "I love you, Lloyd," she murmured against his chest. "I love you so much."

"Oh, God, Delaney," he said. "Help me. Please help me. I feel like I'm falling apart."

Chapter 10

IT WAS DARK by the time the fire burned down far enough for the fire fighters to go inside the charred area and search for survivors. The moment he heard they were going in, Lloyd left the command post to join them. Giant searchlights had been trucked in, and more people had arrived.

"You'll have to stay here, Delaney," Lloyd told her. "Where it's safe."

She nodded, knowing she would only get in the way if she went with him. "I'll wait outside, though, if it's okay."

"Just stay back from the fire."

By this time the firemen were fairly certain that the gas pocket had burned itself out; however, it could flare here or there in a brief but deadly flame. "Be careful," she murmured.

"I'll be fine."

"Lloyd," she whispered, "there's still reason to hope."

But the pain in his eyes had deepened. He hadn't mentioned Curt again, but she knew he was thinking of the boy all the time. He shrugged. "Maybe."

What had happened to the eternal optimist? "Please try. For me?"

He nodded. "Okay."

"I'll be waiting," she said.

Moments later, armed with shovels and first aid equipment, Lloyd followed the small group of fire fighters into the burned-out woods. Smoke rose from the area in dense curls, like fog from a river. Palely illuminated by the searchlights, the entire area resembled a scene from an eerie movie.

Although it seemed like hours, Delaney waited only minutes. Suddenly a whoop came up from beyond a hill. She could hear the echo of excited voices, and wanted to cheer herself. But she stood immobile, praying that she was right, that they had found someone—anyone—alive.

The men came back through the smoke like knights rising from the moors. Everyone was talking at once, laughing and shouting. Bedraggled, soot-covered, and wet, they looked as though they had been through a war. Yet they were jubilant. Lloyd led the way, with Curt leaning against his shoulder. Despite his limp, the young boy was smiling.

"We made it!" he shouted triumphantly, shaking his fist in the air at the people waiting beside the command post. "We did it!"

As he spoke, cameras flashed and whined. Until that moment Delaney had hardly been aware that the reporters were present. "Where did you hide?" someone shouted to the recruits. "How did you escape the fire?"

"They hid from the fire by lying down in the river," Lloyd answered, pushing his way to a stretcher and setting Curt down on it. "Excuse me. We'll have a statement for you later. Right now we need to get these boys some medical attention. Get some stretchers into the woods," he snapped the order to one of the waiting medics.

Several soldiers headed for the woods immediately. A doctor knelt beside Curt. Now that she was up close, Delaney realized the young boy was hurt badly. He had been limping, and the doctor was now examining his legs; he was burned on his arms and on one side of his face. Clumps of his hair were singed.

The reporters must have noticed, too, and they clustered around the boy, asking rapid-fire questions. "How'd you get the other men to the river? Did you know the explosion was coming?"

"He carried most of us," another recruit said. "He pushed and pulled and poked the rest. He's a real hero."

"I didn't do anything special," Curt denied. "I just happened to be there."

"Don't let him tell you that," another recruit spoke up. "He saved us. All of us. It was his idea to head for the river. He made us lie in the water for hours, ducking our heads below the surface when the flames started to scorch the riverbanks."

"Then as soon as we could walk out of the area,"

the first boy broke in, "he mobilized us to get back up here."

"Yeah, he never gave up," someone else said, "and he never let us give up, either. He just kept saying we were going to make it."

"Looks like you *are* a hero," one of the reporters remarked.

"He only did what any other Marine would do," Lloyd said, winking at Curt. Clearly his statement was for the benefit of the reporters.

Curt laughed and nodded toward Lloyd. "This is my recruiting officer."

"We could tell," the reporters said. "So the boy's a Marine, huh?"

"Soon to be one," Lloyd said seriously. "If he's still willing to sign."

Curt laughed. "Show me the papers."

Delaney stood listening, as proud of Curt as she would have been of her own son. He had certainly behaved heroically in this crisis, and while it had been a tragic moment in their lives, perhaps they were all stronger because of it. Delaney suddenly realized that the adversity she'd been struggling against was part of living. Why had it taken her so long to figure that out? Everything that had happened in her life had made her the person she was today, just as the events in Lloyd's life had made him the special man she loved so very much.

A few moments later the men were loaded into ambulances. Lloyd and Delaney accompanied the recruits to the hospital. Most were treated and released; only a few were admitted. After many congratulations, Curt was told he could go home.

"Since I've had so many years of experience as a

mother, I think I'm a better nurse than you," Delaney told Lloyd. "Let's take him to my house."

Lloyd agreed. After the teenager was settled in a spare bedroom, he turned to her, taking her into his arms and nearly crushing her against his chest. "Thanks, Delaney," he said, "for staying with me. I couldn't have gotten through this day without you."

"Oh, Lloyd, you don't have to thank me. I love you."

"I love you, too, babe." He sighed and rubbed her back gently. "I think I know now what you went through all those times you lost people you loved."

"At least Curt's alive."

"Yes, but two other boys are dead."

Delaney could tell he was carrying a burden of guilt. "The accident wasn't your fault, Lloyd. You have to remember that."

"I keep going over things in my mind, wondering if there was any way it could have been prevented."

"I'm sure the Marines don't take a geological survey of every piece of land they own. Even then, the firemen said the natural gas pocket might not have been detected. It was just something that had been building up for thousands of years."

"I know. It was a freak accident. But I have to go see the parents of those dead boys tomorrow. How can I explain that to them?"

He didn't have to go; the official notification had already been made. Lloyd was going to see the parents because he wanted to, because that was the kind of man he was. Delaney didn't envy him the responsibility. "You explain, and you hope they'll understand."

"I suppose."

Fatigue lined his face. She brushed back the lock of hair that fell onto his forehead. "You look tired," she said tenderly.

"It's been a long day."

Too long. "Want to stay here tonight?"

He shook his head. "I better get going. I still have all that paperwork to finish."

And he would have more as a result of this accident, Delaney knew. She wanted to lift the burden from him, but there was nothing she could do. "I love you," she said again.

He kissed her gently. "I'll call you in the morning, okay?"

After he had left, she checked on Curt, who was sound asleep. Exhausted, she went to bed herself. It was hard to believe that just that morning she had been laughing and carefree in Hilton Head Island, South Carolina. How quickly tragedy could strike.

Since Kevin was due home soon, Delaney had arranged for several more days off, and she didn't have to go into work the following day. He arrived in the morning on an early flight. He had gotten his orders and was headed for Camp Lejeune next. Delaney wasn't surprised that Kevin had opted for the infantry. In so many ways he reminded her of Lloyd, and the infantry was one of the toughest assignments in the Marines.

Kevin was duly impressed with Curt's heroism, and the two boys got on splendidly. They talked endlessly about boot camp and life in the military in general. Lloyd called, but Delaney didn't see him until very late that night. He was smiling when he came in, but Delaney could tell he was still upset. It would take more than a few hours to get over a disaster of that kind—if he could ever really get over it.

After dinner she brought lemonade and cookies out onto the front porch and sat beside Lloyd in the swing. The boys had gone out as soon as they had eaten. Curt insisted he felt fine, and Adrienne had persuaded a friend to go out with them. Curt had seemed as excited as a child at Christmastime.

"Look, I brought you cookies and you didn't even have to mow the lawn," Delaney teased, settling next to Lloyd.

He glanced at her and smiled. "I'll get to it tomorrow."

"You're not listening, Lloyd. I said you didn't even have to mow the lawn."

He sighed heavily. "Sorry, I wasn't listening."

She set the cookies aside. "Do you want to talk about it?"

"About what?"

"About whatever's bothering you. Is it the accident?"

"Yes."

"Did you see the parents of the dead boys today?"

"Yes."

This time the word sounded painful as he whispered it. She didn't know what to say; he already knew he wasn't at fault.

He sighed again. "Delaney, I'm going to try to talk Curt out of joining the Marines."

She looked at him in surprise. "Curt's pretty adamant about going."

"Especially now," Lloyd agreed. "He was a natural leader yesterday during the accident. A lot of boys looked up to him, but I'm still hoping I can talk him into going to college instead or getting a job or doing something else—anything but the service."

"But why?" Delaney was truly shocked now. "Because of this—the accident?"

"He could have been killed."

"But he *wasn't* killed, Lloyd. He's alive and he's looking forward to joining the Marines."

He glanced at her warily. "You've certainly changed your tune. When I met you, you were vehemently opposed to the military."

She shrugged. "I guess I have changed. A person can die crossing the street, Lloyd. I think you pointed that out to me the day we met."

"The chances of dying are certainly higher with a military career."

"Not necessarily. This is peacetime."

"Death is final, peacetime or wartime."

"It's also final whether you're a soldier or a civilian. What about the things the military has given you, Lloyd? You've had opportunities—"

"What about the things it's taken away from me?" he cut in. "I've lived a solitary life. I've sacrificed things other men take for granted—a wife, a family, stability."

"Lloyd, lots of people in the military have those things. You can't blame the Marines because you didn't meet a woman right after your divorce."

"But I can blame the military for my divorce."

She hesitated. She didn't want to hurt him. But this was the time to speak the truth. "I thought Amy chose not to be with you."

"Yes, that's true." He sighed. "Speaking of marriage . . . how would you like to be married to a carpenter? I think I can get a job on the outside with a construction crew."

She frowned at him. "What about reenlisting?"

"I've decided not to reenlist."

Lloyd had changed his mind? It was incomprehensible to Delaney.

"We won't have to worry about being transferred," he went on, pointing out the advantages. "It'll all be local work."

Her frown deepened. "Lloyd, are you saying you're doing this for me? You're sacrificing the Marines so we can stay near Chicago?"

"No, I'm doing this for me. But I know how you feel about the military."

"You don't know anything about carpentry."

"I can learn."

"Can you? You're almost forty years old. Can you start a new career just like that?"

"Lots of men retire at forty and start new careers."

"Men like you? Men who are dedicated to the service?" Delaney had to do something, think of something to help him through this crisis. Quitting the Marines would be the worst mistake of his life. And no matter what the military had done to Delaney, it had also given her Lloyd. Now it might take him away from her. She would lose Lloyd as surely as she had lost everyone else. "Look," she went on abruptly, "can we go for a ride?"

He gave her an odd glance. "Where do you want to go?"

"Lovers' lane."

"Delaney, I—"

"I don't want to make out," she said. "I just want to go for a walk around the lake."

"The lake?"

"Yes, the lake," she said impatiently. "Can we go?"

He shrugged. "Why not."

"I'll drive," she said.

Delaney had no idea what she was going to say to him when they got to lovers' lane. She just knew she had to do something to help him. She had already lost too many people she cared about—this time she wasn't going to lose!

Lovers' lane was crowded for a weekday. Several cars were lined up in a neat row, their parking lights lit. Delaney and Lloyd got out of the car and started to walk hand in hand beside the lake.

It was another soft, moonlit night, similar to the first time they had come. But now it was fall and there was a harvest moon. The lake was smooth and glassy. Here and there a ripple marred the surface, making its way slowly to shore.

They sat on the bench. Delaney gestured toward the opposite shore where the stream fed into the lake. "I think the beavers have multiplied," she said. "There seem to be a few more dams."

"Industrious little creatures."

"Pain is a fact of life, Lloyd."

He glanced at her. "How'd we get from beavers to pain?"

"I'm tired of skirting the issue. A person has to take risks—every day. Every single solitary day is a risk, just getting up in the morning. When you stop taking risks, you're dead inside. Lloyd, you taught me that. Why can't you see it now?"

"I guess because I've taken a risk and lost."

"Look," she went on, trying another tack. "A few

months ago you brought me out here after Kevin left for the Marines. We were talking about the beaver—"

"It's a cold, cruel world, even for beavers?" he cut in, repeating her words.

"Yes, that's what I said, and that's how I felt at the time, and I know that's how you feel right now. But what you said then was right. We were talking about death and dying and growing up. We didn't say it, but that's what we were talking about. All you wanted to do was help me accept what was happening. Lloyd, now you have to accept that there are some things you don't have any control over. You'll always get hurt, but you have to go on. You gave me the will to go on. You showed me how to live again, Lloyd. Can't you understand that?"

"I think so." He frowned.

She took his hands and spoke earnestly. "What can I do to help you, Lloyd? Please tell me; share this with me."

For a long moment he didn't say anything. Then he whispered raggedly, "Oh, God, Delaney, the pain is like a ball of fire inside me."

"If it's any comfort, it gets easier," she said softly. "Every day it gets more and more bearable."

"I feel so helpless."

"In the general scheme of things I suppose we're all pretty helpless," she murmured, almost to herself. Then she turned back to Lloyd. She loved him so very much.

"I didn't handle this very well," Lloyd said soberly.

"Strength is more than muscles, Lloyd. You're still strong. You're the strongest person I know. You just have to learn to accept the things you can't change."

"Like death."

"And life," she said. "The things that happen to us."

"Seems kind of cruel right now."

She went on gently, "You happened to me, Lloyd. And I never, ever want to change that."

Smiling, he gathered her close. "I love you, Delaney."

"Oh, Lloyd, I love you."

"Do you think we'll make it?"

"Yes, I do." She pulled away with a sigh, tracing her thumb across his lips. "One more thing."

"What's that?"

"You can't quit the Marines and become a carpenter."

"It'll be easier, Delaney. We'll have a better life."

She shook her head adamantly. "You're giving up the Marines for all the wrong reasons. I don't want you to do this for me, or for Curt or for anyone but yourself. If you want to quit, fine. But don't do it for us. You're my hero, Lloyd. And you'll make a great major."

"Even if we have to move?"

"Even if."

"Even if we have to live on a base?"

"Yes."

He paused before he asked the most painful question. "Even if something happens to me?"

The words were hard for her to say. "Yes," she whispered. "Even if."

In the distance a beaver splashed. Lloyd took her in his arms and kissed her. "Let's go home, Delaney

Anderson. Lovers' lane is no place for a lady. And we've got a big job ahead of us."

"What's that?"

"Making a baby."

She smiled. "I thought we already proved in South Carolina that I'm not a lady."

"You're a wanton woman, then, and lovers' lane is no place for a wanton woman."

"You're spoiled, Captain Lloyd Thomas, especially for a Marine. I'm beginning to think you always need a bed."

He laughed. "I suppose you're ready to make love right here? Want to go behind the beaver dams?"

She glanced around thoughtfully. "Do beavers peek?"

"I don't know." He laughed again and grabbed her hand, pulling her alongside him. "But what the hell, let's find out."

"Lloyd!"

Pausing, he kissed her briefly. "What? Are you backing out now?"

"Maybe. Yes."

"Come on, Delaney, let's take a chance."

"Right here?" It was so good to have him back, this laughing, carefree Lloyd.

"Right here."

"What if somebody comes?"

"We're adults, and we'll be behind the beaver dams."

"Lloyd! I don't believe this," she said as he led her down the path into the dark, wooded area. "I don't believe I'm doing this."

"Believe it," he said, drawing her down onto the soft ground. Just before his lips met hers, he murmured, "Believe it. And believe in us."

SECOND CHANCE AT LOVE

COMING NEXT MONTH

SECOND CHANCE AT LOVE

Be Sure to Read These New Releases!

NO HOLDS BARRED #394 by Jackie Leigh
Eli Sutherland's content being an investment
manager by day and wrestler Stud Savage by night...
until Kate Harcourt begins playing Stud's "girlfriend" and
turns his carefully planned life topsy-turvy.

DEVIN'S PROMISE #395 by Kelly Adams
Twelve years after their shared youth, the roguish,
irrepressible Devin O'Neill is back for good—
and Cass Heath's determined not to lose her heart
again to this Irish charmer...

FOR LOVE OF CHRISTY #396 by Jasmine Craig
When policewoman Laura Forbes marries America's
sexiest heartthrob, TV superstar Bennett Logan, to help
him win custody of his daughter Christy, their
marriage of convenience proves to be anything but!

WHISTLING DIXIE #397 by Adrienne Edwards
Engaged in an amorous battle, snake curator
Roberta E. Lee's determined not to surrender—but
Yankee banker Stephen Grant's planning
strategies guaranteed to besiege her southern heart.

BEST INTENTIONS #398 by Sherryl Woods
Tough-talking Traci Marie's got things under control—
until her freewheeling ex-husband Doug Maguire comes back
to see his son, charming his way into her heart...

NIGHT MOVES #399 by Jean Kent
When Drug Enforcement Administration officer Greg
Heflin investigates Kelsey Sviderskas, he finds himself
falling for this trusting Swedish beauty—
or is he falling for a clever innocence act?

Order on opposite page

SECOND CHANCE AT LOVE

___ 0-425-09610-6	HANKY-PANKY #371 Jan Mathews	$2.25
___ 0-425-09611-4	PROUD SURRENDER #372 Jackie Leigh	$2.25
___ 0-425-09612-2	ALMOST HEAVEN #373 Lee Williams	$2.25
___ 0-425-09613-0	FIRE AND ICE #374 Carol Katz	$2.25
___ 0-425-09614-9	ALL FOR LOVE #375 Sherryl Woods	$2.25
___ 0-425-09690-0	WHEN LIGHTNING STRIKES #376 Martina Sultan	$2.25
___ 0-425-09691-9	TO CATCH A THIEF #377 Diana Morgan	$2.25
___ 0-425-09692-0	ON HER DOORSTEP #378 Kay Robbins	$2.25
___ 0-425-09693-9	VIOLETS ARE BLUE #379 Hilary Cole	$2.25
___ 0-425-09694-7	A SWEET DISORDER #380 Katherine Granger	$2.25
___ 0-425-09695-5	MORNING GLORY #381 Kasey Adams	$2.25
___ 0-425-09741-2	FIRE UNDER HEAVEN #382 Cinda Richards	$2.25
___ 0-425-09742-0	LADY INCOGNITO #383 Courtney Ryan	$2.25
___ 0-425-09743-9	SOFTER THAN SPRINGTIME #384 Frances West	$2.25
___ 0-425-09744-7	A HINT OF SCANDAL #385 Dana Daniels	$2.25
___ 0-425-09745-5	CUPID'S VERDICT #386 Jackie Leigh	$2.25
___ 0-425-09746-3	CHANGE OF HEART #387 Helen Carter	$2.25
___ 0-425-09831-1	PLACES IN THE HEART #388 Delaney Devers	$2.25
___ 0-425-09832-X	A DASH OF SPICE #389 Kerry Price	$2.25
___ 0-425-09833-8	TENDER LOVING CARE #390 Jeanne Grant	$2.25
___ 0-425-09834-6	MOONSHINE AND MADNESS #391 Kate Gilbert	$2.25
___ 0-425-09835-4	MADE FOR EACH OTHER #392 Aimee Duvall	$2.25
___ 0-425-09836-2	COUNTRY DREAMING #393 Samantha Quinn	$2.25
___ 0-425-09943-1	NO HOLDS BARRED #394 Jackie Leigh	$2.25
___ 0-425-09944-X	DEVIN'S PROMISE #395 Kelly Adams	$2.25
___ 0-425-09945-8	FOR LOVE OF CHRISTY #396 Jasmine Craig	$2.25
___ 0-425-09946-6	WHISTLING DIXIE #397 Adrienne Edwards	$2.25
___ 0-425-09947-4	BEST INTENTIONS #398 Sherryl Woods	$2.25
___ 0-425-09948-2	NIGHT MOVES #399 Jean Kent	$2.25
___ 0-425-10048-0	IN NAME ONLY #400 Mary Modean	$2.25
___ 0-425-10049-9	RECLAIM THE DREAM #401 Liz Grady	$2.25
___ 0-425-10050-2	CAROLINA MOON #402 Joan Darling	$2.25
___ 0-425-10051-0	THE WEDDING BELLE #403 Diana Morgan	$2.25
___ 0-425-10052-9	COURTING TROUBLE #404 Laine Allen	$2.25
___ 0-425-10053-7	EVERYBODY'S HERO #405 Jan Mathews	$2.25

Available at your local bookstore or return this form to:

SECOND CHANCE AT LOVE
THE BERKLEY PUBLISHING GROUP, Dept. B
390 Murray Hill Parkway, East Rutherford, NJ 07073

Please send me the titles checked above. I enclose _____ Include $1.00 for postage
and handling if one book is ordered; add 25¢ per book for two or more not to exceed
$1.75. CA, IL, NJ, NY, PA, and TN residents please add sales tax. Prices subject to change
without notice and may be higher in Canada.

NAME _____

ADDRESS _____

CITY _____ STATE/ZIP _____

(Allow six weeks for delivery.)   SK-41b